# RONESA AVEELA

# DRAGON TALES
## from Eastern Europe

BENDIDEIA
PUBLISHING

# CONTENTS

# Contents

# HERE BE DRAGONS

This book is a collection of fairy tales from Eastern Europe. Not any fairy tales, but ones with and about dragons. In many of the hero tales that have been passed down generation after generation, defeating dragons is only one part of the hero's quest. So, if you don't see a dragon right away in any one story, read on. One or more will be lurking within the pages.

We've edited many of the stories from the sources we've used, replacing words such as "thee" and "thou" with "you." And, although Poe's raven may prefer "quoth," we thought "said" would be more familiar to your ears.

Giant snakes were also representations of dragons in some stories. We've taken the liberty to change the word "snake" to "dragon" within these tales, but the intent is still the same.

In addition, over the years, some stories have gained religious references. We've removed the majority of these, not because we are anti-religion (because we're not), but to make the stories more suitable to a broader audience. Where a religious aspect was part of the story, we retained the references.

Although some events are repetitive from story to story, we didn't want to choose between including them. Each tale has its own merits, and so in a few instances, you'll discover similar tales told in different manners.

If you enjoy this book and would like to learn more about dragons, check out our nonfiction book on the subject: *A Study of Dragons of Eastern Europe*, https://books2read.com/dragons-aveela.

Without further ado, we'll leave you to enjoy these tales of old.

# VITAZKO THE VICTORIOUS

There was once a mother who had an only son. "He'll be a hero," she said, "and his name will be Vitazko, the Victorious."

She nursed him for twice seven years. Then, to try his strength, she led him into the forest and told him to pull up a fir tree by its roots.

The boy wasn't strong enough to do this, so she took him home and nursed him for another seven years. Then, when she had nursed him for three times seven years, she led him into the forest again and ordered him to pull up a beech tree by its roots.

The youth grasped the tree, and, with one mighty pull, uprooted it.

"My son, you're strong enough," the mother said, "and worthy of your name Vitazko, for now you will be victorious. Don't forget the mother who's nursed you for three times seven years. Since you're grown, it's time for you to take care of her."

"I will, my mother," Vitazko promised. "Please tell me what you want me to do."

"First," the mother said, "go into the world and find me a splendid dwelling where I may live in peace and plenty."

Taking in his hand the uprooted beech tree as a club and armed only with it, Vitazko set forth. He followed the wind here and there and the other place, and it led him at last to a fine castle. Dragons lived there. Vitazko pounded on the gates, but the dragons refused to let him in. Therefore, the young hero battered down the gates, pursued the dragons from room to room, and slaughtered them all.

When he had thrown the last of them over the wall, he took possession of the castle. He found nine spacious chambers and a tenth one, the door of which was closed.

Vitazko opened the door, and in the room, he found another dragon. This one was a prisoner. Three iron hoops were fastened about his body, and these were chained to the wall.

"Oho!" Vitazko cried. "Another dragon! What are you doing here?"

1

"Me?" the dragon said. "I'm not doing anything, but just sitting here. My brothers imprisoned me. Unchain me, Vitazko! If you do, I'll reward you richly."

"I won't!" Vitazko said. "A fine scamp you must be if your own brothers had to chain you up! No! You stay where you are!"

With that, Vitazko slammed the door in the dragon's face and left him. Then he went for his mother and brought her to the castle.

"Here, my mother," he said, "is the dwelling I've won for you."

He took her through the nine spacious chambers and showed her everything. At the tenth door, he said, "Don't open this door. All the castle belongs to you except this room. See to it you never open this door. If you do, you'll suffer an evil fate."

Then Vitazko took his beech club and went out hunting.

He was hardly gone before his mother sat in front of the tenth door and said to herself over and over, "I wonder what's in that room? Why doesn't Vitazko want me to open the door?"

At last, when she could restrain her curiosity no longer, she opened the door.

"Mercy on us!" she said when she saw the dragon. "Who are you? And what are you doing here?"

"Me?" the dragon said. "I'm only a poor harmless dragon. They call me Sharkan. My brothers chained me here. They would have freed me long ago, but Vitazko killed them. Unchain me, dear lady, and I'll reward you richly."

He begged and cajoled her until she was half minded to do as he asked.

"You're very beautiful," Sharkan said. "If only I were free, I'd make you my wife."

"But what would Vitazko say to that?" the woman asked.

"Vitazko?" repeated Sharkan. "Do you fear your own son? A dutiful son he is, to give you the castle and then forbid you to enter this room! If you were to marry me, we'd soon get rid of this Vitazko, and then live here together in peace and festivity."

The woman listened to these cajoling words until she was completely won over. "But how, dear Sharkan, can I unchain you?"

He told her to go to the cellar and from a certain cask to draw him a goblet of wine. Instantly, he drank the wine. *Bang!* The first iron hoop burst open. He drank a second goblet, and the second iron hoop fell from him. He drank a third goblet and, at last, he was free.

Then in dismay at what she had done, the woman cried, "Ah me, what will Vitazko say when he comes home?"

"I've thought out a plan," Sharkan said. "Listen: when he comes home, pretend you're sick and refuse to eat. He'll beg you to eat something, but tell him that nothing can tempt you except a piglet from the Earth Sow. He'll go at once and hunt the Earth Sow, but when he touches one of her piglets, the Sow will tear him to pieces."

Sharkan remained in hiding in the tenth chamber, and presently Vitazko returned from the hunt with a young buck across his shoulders. He found his mother on the bed, moaning and groaning as if in great pain.

"What is it, dear mother?" he asked. "Are you sick?"

"Yes, my son, I'm sick. Leave me, and let me die alone!"

Vitazko, in alarm, rubbed her hands and begged her to eat of the venison he'd brought home.

"No, my son," she said, "venison doesn't tempt me. Nothing can ease my waning appetite except a piglet from the Earth Sow."

"Then, my mother, you'll have a piglet from the Earth Sow!" Vitazko cried. Immediately, he rushed out in quest of the Earth Sow and her litter.

With his beech tree in his hand, he trekked through the forest, hunting the Earth Sow. He came at last to a tower in which an old wise woman lived. Her name was Nedyelka. Because she was good as well as wise, people called her St. Nedyelka.

"Where are you going, Vitazko?" she said when she saw the young hero.

"I'm hunting for the Earth Sow," he told her. "My mother is sick, and nothing will tempt her but a piglet from the Earth Sow's litter."

Nedyelka looked at the young man kindly.

"That, my son, is a difficult task you've undertaken. However, I'll help you, provided you do exactly as I say."

Vitazko promised, and the old woman gave him a long-pointed spit.

"Take this," she said. "Now go to my stable. There you'll find my horse, Tatosh. Mount him, and he'll carry you on the wind to where the Earth Sow lies half buried in her wallow and surrounded by her litter. Reach over and prick one of the piglets with this spit and then sit still without moving. The piglet will squeal, and instantly the Sow will spring up and in a fury. She'll race madly around the world and back in a moment of time. Sit perfectly still, and she won't see either you or Tatosh. Then she'll tell the litter that if one of them squeals again and disturbs her, she'll tear it to pieces. With that, she'll settle back in the wallow and go to sleep. Then you can pick up the same piglet on your spit and carry it off. This time, it'll be afraid to squeal. The Sow won't be disturbed, and Tatosh will carry you safely away."

Vitazko did exactly as Nedyelka ordered. He mounted Tatosh, and the magic steed carried him swiftly on the wind to where the Earth Sow lay sleeping in her wallow.

With his spit, Vitazko pricked one of the piglets until it squealed in terror. The Earth Sow jumped up, and, in fury, raced madly around the world and back in a moment of time. Tatosh stood where he was, and Vitazko sat on his back without moving. The Earth Sow saw neither of them.

"If one of you squeals again and disturbs me," the Earth Sow said to the litter, "I'll wake up and tear you to pieces!"

With that, she settled back into the mud and fell asleep.

Vitazko again reached over and picked up the same piglet on the end of his spit. This time, it made no sound. Instantly, Tatosh, the magic steed, rose on the wind and flew straight home to Nedyelka.

"How did things go?" the old woman asked.

"Just as you said they would," Vitazko told her. "See, here is the piglet."

"Good, my son. Take it home to your mother."

Vitazko returned the spit and led Tatosh back to his stall. Then he threw the piglet over his beech tree, thanked old St. Nedyelka, bade her good day, and, with a happy heart, went home.

At the castle, his mother was laughing and having fun with the dragon. Suddenly, in the distance, they saw Vitazko returning.

"Here he comes!" the mother cried. "Oh dear, what can I do?"

"Don't be afraid," Sharkan advised. "We'll send him off on another quest. This time, he'll surely not come back. Pretend you're sick again and tell him you're so weak that even the piglet of the Earth Sow doesn't tempt your appetite. Tell him nothing will help you except the Water of Life and the Water of Death, and, if he really loves you, he must get you some of both. Then he'll go off hunting the Water of Life and the Water of Death, and that will be the end of him."

Sharkan hid himself in the tenth chamber, and Vitazko, when he entered the castle, found his mother alone.

"It's no use, my son," she moaned. "I can't eat the piglet. Nothing will help me now except the Water of Life and the Water of Death. Of course, you don't love me well enough to get me some of both."

"I do! I do!" poor Vitazko cried. "There's nothing I won't get for you to make you well!"

He snatched up his beech tree again and hurried back to St. Nedyelka.

"What is it now?" the old woman asked.

"Can you tell me, dear St. Nedyelka, where I can find the Water of Life and the Water of Death? My poor mother is still sick, and she says that nothing else will cure her."

"The Waters of Life and Death are difficult to get," Nedyelka said. "However, dear boy, I'll help you. Take these two pitchers and again

4

mount the faithful Tatosh. He'll carry you to the two shores under which flow the springs of the Water of Life and the Water of Death. The right shore opens for a moment at exactly noon, and under it the Water of Life bubbles up. The left shore opens for a moment at midnight, and under it lies the still pool of the Water of Death. Wait at each shore until the moment it opens. Then reach in and scoop up a pitcher of water. Be swift, or the shores will close on you and kill you."

Vitazko took the two pitchers and mounted Tatosh. The horse rose on the wind and carried Vitazko far, far away beyond the Red Sea to the two shores of which old Nedyelka had told him.

At precisely noon, the right shore opened for an instant, and Vitazko scooped up a pitcher of the Water of Life. He had scarcely time to draw back before the opening closed with a crash.

He waited at the left shore until midnight. At precisely midnight, the left shore opened for an instant. Vitazko scooped up a pitcher of water from the still pool of the Water of Death and pulled swiftly back as the opening closed.

With the two pitchers safe in his hands, Vitazko mounted Tatosh, and the magic steed, rising on the wind, carried him home to St. Nedyelka.

"And how did things go?" the old woman asked.

"Very well," Vitazko said. "See, here are the Waters."

St. Nedyelka took the two pitchers and, when Vitazko wasn't looking, changed them for two pitchers of ordinary water, which she told him to carry at once to his mother.

At the castle, the mother and Sharkan were again laughing and having fun, when from the distance, they saw Vitazko with two pitchers in his hands. The mother fell into a great fright, wept, and tore her hair, but the dragon again reassured her.

"He's come back this time," he said, "but we'll send him off again, and he'll never return. Refuse the Waters and tell him you're so sick that nothing will help you now except a sight of the bird Pelikan. Tell him if he loves you, he'll go after the bird. Once he goes, we need never fear him again."

Vitazko, when he reached the castle, hurried into his mother's chamber and offered her the Waters.

"Here, dear mother, is a pitcher of the Water of Life and a pitcher of the Water of Death. Now you'll get well!"

But his mother pushed both pitchers away. Moaning and groaning as if she were in great pain, she said, "No, you're too late with your Water of Life and your Water of Death! I'm so far gone that nothing will cure me now except a sight of the bird Pelikan. If you really loved me, you'd get it for me."

Vitazko, still trusting his mother, cried out, "Of course, I love you! Of course, I'll get you the bird Pelikan, if that's what will cure you!"

So once more, he snatched up his beech tree and hurried off to St. Nedyelka.

"What is it now?" the old woman asked him.

"It's my poor mother," Vitazko said. "She's too far gone for the Water of Life and the Water of Death. Nothing will help her now except a sight of the bird Pelikan. Tell me, kind Nedyelka, how can I get the bird?"

"The bird Pelikan, my son? Ah, that's quite a task to capture him! However, I'll help you. Pelikan is a giant bird with a long, long neck. When he shakes his wings, he raises such a wind that he blows down the forest trees. Here's a gun. Take it and mount my faithful Tatosh. He'll carry you far away to the vast wilderness where Pelikan lives. When you get there, note carefully from what direction the wind blows. Shoot in that direction. Then quickly push the ramrod into the barrel of the gun and leave it there and come back to me as fast as you can."

Vitazko took the gun and mounted Tatosh. The magic steed rose on the wind and carried him far off to the distant wilderness, which was the home of the bird Pelikan. There Tatosh sank to earth, and Vitazko dismounted. Immediately, he felt a strong wind against his right cheek. He took aim in that direction and pulled the trigger. The hammer fell, and instantly Vitazko pushed the ramrod into the gun barrel. He threw the gun over his shoulder and mounted Tatosh. The steed rose on the wind and, in a twinkling, had carried him back to St. Nedyelka.

"Well, son, how did things go?" the old woman asked as usual.

"I don't know," Vitazko said. "I did as you told me. Here's the gun."

"Let me see," Nedyelka said, squinting into the gun barrel. "Ah, son, things went very well indeed! Here is Pelikan inside the barrel."

She drew something out of the gun barrel, and, sure enough, it was the bird Pelikan.

She gave Vitazko another gun and told him to go out and shoot an eagle. Then she told him to carry Pelikan home to his mother, but instead of giving him Pelikan, she gave him the eagle.

When Sharkan and his mother saw Vitazko coming, they decided that this time they would send him after the Golden Apples. These grew in the garden of the most powerful dragon in the world.

"If Vitazko goes near him," Sharkan said, "the dragon will tear him to pieces, because he knows it was Vitazko who killed all his brother dragons."

The mother again feigned sickness and, when Vitazko rushed in to her and offered her what he supposed was Pelikan, she moaned and groaned and pushed the bird aside.

6

"Too late! Too late! I'm dying!"

"Don't say that!" poor Vitazko begged. "Will nothing save you?"

"Yes, the Golden Apples that grow in the garden of the Mightiest Dragon could still save me. If you really loved me, you'd get them for me."

"I do love you, mother," Vitazko cried, "and I'll get you the Golden Apples wherever they are!"

Without a moment's rest, he hurried back to St. Nedyelka.

"Well, son, what is it now?" the old woman asked.

Vitazko wept. "It's my poor mother. She's still sick. Pelikan hasn't cured her. She says now that only the Golden Apples from the garden of the Mightiest Dragon can cure her. Dear, kind Nedyelka, tell me, what can I do?"

"The Golden Apples from the garden of the Mightiest Dragon! Ah, my son, that'll be quite a task for you. For this, you'll need every ounce of your strength and more. But don't worry. I'll help you again. Here's a ring. Put it on a finger on your right hand. When you're in great trouble, twist the ring around your finger and think of me. Instantly, you'll have the strength of a hundred fighting men. Now take this sword, mount the faithful Tatosh, and good luck go with you."

Vitazko thanked the dear old woman, mounted Tatosh, and was soon carried far away to the garden of the dragon. A high wall surrounded the garden, so high that Vitazko could never have scaled it alone. But it's as easy for a horse like Tatosh to take a high wall as it is for a bird.

Inside the garden, Vitazko dismounted and began to look for the tree that bore the Golden Apples. Presently, he met a beautiful young girl, who asked him what he was doing in the dragon's garden.

"I'm looking for the Golden Apples," he told her. "I want some of them for my sick mother. Do you know where they are?"

"I do, indeed, know where they are," the girl said. "It's my duty to guard them. If I were to give you one, the wicked dragon would tear me to pieces. I'm a royal princess, but I'm in the dragon's power and must do as he says. Dear youth, take my advice and escape while you can. If the dragon sees you, he'll kill you as he would a fly."

But Vitazko wouldn't be dissuaded from his quest. "No, sweet princess, I must get the apples."

"Well, then," she said, "I'll help you if I can. Here's a precious ring. Put it on a finger of your left hand. When you're in great trouble, think of me and twist the ring. You'll have the strength of a hundred men, but to conquer this horrible monster, you'll need the strength of more than a hundred."

Vitazko put on the ring, thanked the princess, and marched boldly on. In the center of the garden, he found the tree that bore the Golden Apples. Under it,, lay the dragon himself.

Upon seeing Vitazko, the dragon raised his head and bellowed, "Ho, you murderer of dragons, what do you want here?"

Not daunted, Vitazko replied, "I've come to shake down some of the Golden Apples."

"Indeed!" the dragon roared. "Then you'll have to shake them down over my dead body!"

"I'll be glad to do that!" Vitazko said, springing at the dragon and, at the same time, twisting around the ring on his right hand and thinking of kind old St. Nedyelka.

The dragon grappled with Vitazko and, for a moment, almost took him off his feet. Then Vitazko plunged the dragon into the earth up to his ankles.

Just then, there was the rustling of wings overhead and a black raven cawed out, "Which of you wants my help, you, O Mightiest Dragon, or you, Vitazko, the Victorious?"

"Help me!" the dragon roared.

"What will you give me?"

"As much gold as you want."

"No, raven," Vitazko shouted, "help me, and I'll give you all the dragon's horses that are grazing over there in the meadow."

"Very well, Vitazko," the raven croaked. "I'll help you. What should I do?"

"Cool me when I'm hot," Vitazko said, "when the dragon breathes on me his fiery breath."

They grappled again, and the dragon plunged Vitazko into the ground up to his ankles. Twisting the ring on his right hand and thinking of St. Nedyelka, Vitazko gripped the dragon around the waist and plunged him into the earth up to his knees. They paused for breath, and the raven, which had dipped its wings into a fountain, sat on Vitazko's head and shook down drops of cool water onto his heated face.

Vitazko twisted the ring on his left hand, thought of the beautiful princess, and fought with the dragon again. This time, with a mighty effort, he gripped the dragon as if he were a stake of wood and drove him into the ground up to his shoulders. Then quickly drawing Nedyelka's sword, he cut off the dragon's head.

At once, the lovely princess came running and herself plucked two of the Golden Apples and gave them to Vitazko. She thanked him prettily for rescuing her, and she said to him, "You've saved me, Vitazko, from this fierce monster, and now I'm yours if you want me."

"I do want you, dear princess," Vitazko said, "and, if I could, I'd go with you at once to your father to ask for you in marriage. But I cannot. I must hurry home to my sick mother. If you love me, wait for me a year and a day, and I'll surely return."

The princess made him this promise, and they parted.

Remembering the raven, Vitazko rode over to the meadow and slaughtered the dragon's horses. Then rising on Tatosh, he flew home on the wind to St. Nedyelka.

"Well, son, how did things go?" the old woman asked.

"Gloriously!" Vitazko answered, showing her the Golden Apples. "But if the princess hadn't given me a second ring, I might have been beaten."

"Take home the Golden Apples to your mother," Nedyelka said, "and this time, ride Tatosh to the castle."

So Vitazko mounted Tatosh again and flew to the castle.

Sharkan and his mother were laughing and having fun when they saw him coming.

"Here he comes again!" the mother cried. "What can I do? What can I do?"

But Sharkan could think of nothing further to suggest. Without a word, he hurried to the tenth chamber, where he hid himself, and the woman had to meet Vitazko as best as she could.

She lay on the bed, feigning still to be sick. When Vitazko appeared, she greeted him most affectionately. "My dear son, back again? And safe and sound? Thank God!"

When he gave her the Golden Apples, she jumped up from the bed, pretending that the mere sight of them had cured her.

"Ah, my dear son!" she cried, patting him and caressing him as she used to when he was a child. "What a hero you are!"

She prepared food and feasted him royally. Vitazko ate and was happy his mother was herself again.

When he could eat no more, she took a strong woolen cord and, as if in play, she said to him, "Lie down, my son, and let me bind you with this cord as once I bound your father. Let me see if you're as strong as he was and able to break the cord."

Vitazko smiled and lay down and allowed his mother to bind him with the woolen cord. Then he stretched his muscles and burst the cord into bits.

"Ah, you are strong!" his mother said. "But come, let me try again with a thin silken cord."

Suspecting nothing, Vitazko allowed his mother to bind him hand and foot with a thin silken cord. Then, when he stretched his muscles, the cord cut into his flesh. He lay there, helpless as an infant.

"Sharkan! Sharkan!" the mother called.

The dragon rushed in with a sword, cut off Vitazko's head, and hacked his body into small pieces. He picked out Vitazko's heart and hung it by a string from a beam in the ceiling.

Then the woman gathered together the pieces of her son's body, tied them in a bundle, and fastened the bundle onto Tatosh, who was still waiting below in the courtyard.

"You carried him when he was alive," she said. "Take him now that he's dead. I don't care where."

Tatosh rose on the wind and flew home to St. Nedyelka.

The old wise woman, who knew already what had happened, was waiting for him. She took the pieces of the body from the bundle and washed them in the Water of Death. Then she arranged them piece by piece as they should be, and they grew together until the wounds disappeared and not even a tiny scar remained. After that, she sprinkled the body with the Water of Life and, wonder of wonders, life returned to Vitazko. He stood, well and healthy.

"Ah," he said, rubbing his eyes, "I've been asleep, haven't I?"

"Yes," Nedyelka said, "and if it weren't for me, you'd never have awakened. How do you feel, my son?"

"All right," Vitazko said, "except a little strange, as if I had no heart."

"You have none," Nedyelka told him. "Your heart hangs by a string from a crossbeam in the castle."

She told him what had happened, how his mother had betrayed him, and how Sharkan had cut him into pieces.

Vitazko listened, but he could feel neither surprise nor grief nor anger nor anything. How could he feel, since he had no heart?

"You need your heart, my son," Nedyelka said. "You must go after it."

She disguised him as an old village piper and gave him a pair of bagpipes.

"Go to the castle," she told him, "and play on these pipes. When they offer to reward you, ask for the heart that hangs by a string from the ceiling."

Vitazko took the bagpipes and went to the castle. He played under the castle windows, and his mother looked out and beckoned him in.

He went inside and played, and Sharkan and his mother danced to his music. They danced and danced until they could dance no longer. Then they gave the old piper food and drink and offered him golden money.

But Vitazko said, "No, what use has an old man for gold?"

"What can I give you then?" the woman asked.

Vitazko looked slowly around the chamber as an old man would.

"Give me that heart," he said, "that hangs from the ceiling. That's all I want."

They gave him the heart, and Vitazko thanked them and departed.

He carried the heart to Nedyelka, who washed it at once in the Water of Death and the Water of Life. Then she placed it into the bill of the bird Pelikan, who, reaching its long thin neck down Vitazko's throat, put the heart in its proper place. The heart began to beat, and instantly Vitazko could again feel joy and pain and grief and happiness.

"Now can you feel?" Nedyelka asked.

"Yes," Vitazko said. "Now, thank God, I can feel again!"

"Pelikan," Nedyelka said, "for this service, you'll be freed. As for you, my son, you must go back to the castle once more and inflict a just punishment. I'll change you into a pigeon. Fly to the castle and there, when you wish to be yourself again, think of me."

Vitazko took the form of a pigeon and, flying to the castle, landed on the windowsill. Inside the castle chamber, he saw his mother caressing Sharkan.

"Look!" she cried. "A pigeon is on the windowsill. Quick! Get your crossbow and shoot it!"

But before the dragon could move, Vitazko stood in the chamber. He seized a sword and, with one mighty blow, cut off the dragon's head.

"And you—you wicked, faithless mother!" he cried. "What am I to do to you?"

His mother fell on her knees and begged for mercy.

"Never fear," Vitazko said. "I won't harm you. Let God be our judge."

He took his mother by the hand and led her into the courtyard. Then he lifted the sword and said, "Now, mother, I'll throw this sword into the air, and may God judge between us which of us has been faithless to the other."

The sword flashed in the air and fell, striking straight to the heart of the guilty mother and killing her.

Vitazko buried her in the courtyard and then returned to St. Nedyelka. He thanked the old woman for all she had done for him. Then, picking up his beech tree club, he started out to find his beautiful princess.

She had long since returned to her father, and many princes and heroes had come seeking her in marriage. She had put them all off, saying she would wed no one for a year and a day.

Then, before the year was up, Vitazko appeared, and she led him at once to her father and said, "This is the man I'll marry, him and none other. He was the one who rescued me from the dragon."

A great wedding feast was spread, and all the country rejoiced that their lovely princess was getting for a husband Vitazko, the Victorious.

# Miklosh and the Magic Queen

*Where it was, or where it was not, there was once in the world a magical kingdom. In the center of that kingdom was a great forest, in the center of the forest was a flowery meadow, in the center of the meadow was a silvery river, and in the center of the silvery river was a velvety island, and in the center of the velvety island was an old well from which I took out a story brought from the Operantsia Sea. Whoever won't listen to the story with attention, or interrupts it without request, may he be struck by lightning as many times as there are sand grains in the Danube and the Tisa.*

There was once a poor man who had as many children as there are trees in the forest or stars in the sky. He had so many that he couldn't find godparents for them.

"Well," he thought, "if I can't find godparents in my own village, the world is wide. Maybe I'll find them somewhere else."

The poor man put a loaf in his basket and went out into the world, but he didn't go far. He met a rich merchant who hadn't as many children as there are lumps on swamp grass.

"Where are you going, poor man?" asked the merchant.

"I'm seeking a godfather for my twins."

"If you'll accept my services, don't trouble yourself by going any farther."

"I'll accept not only with one hand but with both. With the new births in my cabin, I don't care whether the godfather is a gypsy or a pagan, since I can't find one in my village."

The merchant became the godfather of the poor man's twins, a boy and a girl, then he took them home and reared them as his own children.

When it was, when it was not, I can't tell exactly, but it's enough that on a certain day when neither the merchant nor his wife was at home, the brother and sister sat down to play cards. They played until the brother won all of his sister's money, and she began to cry.

"Don't cry," said the brother. "I'll give you back your money and some of my own, too." And he did so.

Again, they played. The dice turned, for luck has wings, and to whom it flies, he is all right. This time the girl was the winner. She won her brother's last coin, but she wasn't tender-hearted; she wouldn't give back the money.

"Give me my money," said the brother.

"I won't do it," answered the girl.

"Didn't I give yours back?"

"What do I care? You were a fool."

"Give it back."

"I won't."

"Then I'll take it."

Word followed word until the brother and sister caught each other by the hair. Then the sister cursed the brother and said, "You're not my brother."

"If you deny me, then I'll deny and curse you," screamed the brother.[1]

At these words a dragon appeared, seized the girl, and carried her away.

The brother couldn't stay at home. He was afraid of his foster parents, and he wanted to find his sister, whom he loved. Therefore, he put on his traveling boots and set out to wander around the world. He traveled across forty-nine kingdoms until he came to a king's castle.

He went to the king and spoke to him as was fitting, "Good day to your majesty."

"Good day to you. What brings you here?"

"I'm looking for work. Will your majesty hire me?"

"You've come at a good time, my son. I need a herder. I'll hire you, and you'll have nothing else to do except take care of three vicious horses. Each morning, you'll go with them across the water to an island, but you must not lead them over a bridge or let them swim through the water. The horses must not have a drop of water on them. Each evening, you must bring them back by the same road and in the same manner."

Well and good, the poor man's son became a horse-herder. In the morning, he drove out the three vicious horses, sat on the mare, and led them to the water. When they came to the edge of the water, he wondered how he could lead them across so they didn't go on a bridge, didn't swim, and didn't have a wet spot on them the size of a small nail. But he needn't have wondered, because the three horses crossed by themselves so that not

---

[1] Common curses were such sayings as "May the devil take you." In this case, that devil is a dragon.

even their feet became wet. There was no wonder in that, for they were magic horses. As true as I live, I was there where they were, and I had my eyes as I have them now.

Miklosh, for that was the name of the poor man's son, took off the horses' bridles, fettered their feet, and let them graze on the silken meadow. Then he lay at the foot of a golden apple tree to sleep for a while. All at once, he heard a beautiful song. Where had it come from? He looked around and saw thirteen snow-white swans flying toward him. They settled on the silken meadow near the golden apple tree, shook themselves, and became maidens.

Twelve of the maidens were beautiful, but the thirteenth was far more beautiful. She went to Miklosh and sat on the silken grass near him.

"You're here, my world beautiful love, Miklosh," said the maiden. "Long have I waited for you to come. My heart has longed for you, and I must tell you this. During the year you serve the king, don't let anyone, not even the king, know I come to meet you. Here is my soft white hand; it will be yours. This silken meadow and the golden apple tree on it will be yours and mine, but if you betray me, you won't see me again on the silken meadow or in any other place."

Our Miklosh promised by all that is in heaven and on earth that he would be as silent as a fish, that he wouldn't say a word to any man.

And who was happier than Miklosh, for who had so beautiful a sweetheart? Every day when he drove the horses to the silken meadow and let them out to graze, the thirteen swans appeared and, shaking themselves, became beautiful maidens.

Upon my word, what came of the affair and what didn't, the king gave a great ball to his household. When he came among the rejoicing people and didn't see Miklosh, he asked, "Where is my dear horse-herder, Miklosh?"

"He's in the corner near the door," said someone.

Then the king saw that Miklosh was alone and as sad as an orphan.

"Well, Miklosh," he said, "how is it that you neither eat nor drink, nor dance when the music is playing?"

"Your majesty," said Miklosh, "I don't dance, because I don't have a suitable partner."

"Don't worry. I'll soon send you a partner."

The king went to his daughter, and said, "My daughter, go to the ball and dance with Miklosh, who guards the magic horses, for he is very sad."

The king's daughter didn't wait to be told twice. One reason was that her feet were itching to dance; the other was that she could dance with Miklosh, who was not a handsome fellow for nothing, and the heart of the princess wasn't stone. She dressed in a minute and went to the ball.

"Miklosh, I'm here," she called. "Come, let's dance."

"I won't dance," said Miklosh, shrugging. "I have a sweetheart a hundred times fairer than you."

The king's daughter, as if she had received a cuff on the ear, drew up her mouth, and, weeping, went to complain to her father.

"Why are you crying?" asked the king.

"Why shouldn't I cry? Why shouldn't I weep? Miklosh says he won't dance with me, because he has a sweetheart a hundred times fairer than I."

"Did he say that?"

"He said nothing else."

"Don't cry, my daughter. I'll make what Miklosh said so bitter to him that he won't say it again."

With that, the king called, "Come forth, Miklosh."

"Here I am," said Miklosh, respectfully.

"Did you tell my daughter that you wouldn't dance with her, because you have a sweetheart a hundred times fairer than she is?"

"What's the use of denying? I did indeed say that to the princess. Come to the island tomorrow at the hour I'll set, and your majesty will see with your own eyes that it's true. My sweetheart is a magic queen."

The king didn't reply, but the next day, to know what was in the affair and what was not, he went to the island.

He saw a magic queen, white as a dove, red as an opening rose, and as beautiful as the dawn, talking to Miklosh. On the silken meadow, twelve other maidens were playing ball with a golden apple.

The magic queen realized she had been betrayed.

"Well, Miklosh," she said, "whether you'll ever see me again or not, God only knows. Since you've betrayed me, I must leave immediately. Wait for me no more on the silken meadow or under the golden apple tree."

She turned to the king and said, "Let not a hair of this young man's head fall. It wasn't for you that I made this silken meadow, not for you that I planted the tree that bears golden apples, but for him."

The magic queen and the twelve maidens shook themselves, became swans, and flew away.

There was a magic queen, there is no magic queen; there was, but there is not. Only then did Miklosh drop his chin. Only then did he shake his head. Where he wasn't sore, he was sorry.

Therefore, he hung the world on his neck with the intention of traveling until he found his magic queen.

Miklosh traveled across forty-nine kingdoms until he came to a magic mill, which was turned by the river of kindness. He saluted the miller, saying, "Good day to you, master miller."

"Good day to you, Miklosh. Where are you going?"

"I'm seeking the magic kingdom. Have you heard of its fame, my friend?"

"Have I heard of it? How could I not? I grind flour for that kingdom. But, Miklosh, as long as the world stands, as you are now, you won't be able to get there. That place is farther from here than the sky is from the earth. But don't worry. I'll fix your problem. A griff bird carries flour from my mill to the magic kingdom. The bird takes two sacks at a time. I'll put you into one sack, and the same weight of flour into the other. The sacks must be the same weight; otherwise, the bird can't carry them."

The miller packed Miklosh into one sack, and into the other, he put an equal weight of flour. When the griff bird came, it took a sack in each claw and rose into the air. The bird couldn't fly rapidly, because it carried a heavier load than usual.

A black cloud was drawing near, and the beautiful magic kingdom was still far away. The griff bird flew faster and faster, but the black cloud overtook the bird. Rain fell as if it were poured from a cask. The sack holding the flour became heavier than the other sack. That side of the griff bird sank lower and lower.

What could the bird do? It couldn't carry the two sacks to the magic kingdom. It put down the lighter one in a great wild wood and went on with the other.

Miklosh was in trouble. He took out his shining knife, cut the sack open, and went into the great wild wood. He traveled on and on until he came to a tree under which a youth was sleeping. He nudged the youth with his foot to rouse him. The youth sat up at once.

When he saw Miklosh, he said, "You've come, my dear master. I've waited a long time. Even if you don't say it, still I know where you're going. Follow me. I'll lead you where your heart desires."

The youth led Miklosh to a great forge. "Is the master at home?" asked the youth.

"I'm here," answered the blacksmith.

"Can you make for us twenty-four pairs of iron shoes and twenty-four pairs of iron gloves, twelve pairs for my master and twelve for me?"

While the blacksmith was making the gloves and shoes, Miklosh and his armor-bearer, for Miklosh made him that, went into the blacksmith's house, where his wife, who it may be said, was a witch, busied herself with getting food and drink for her guests. Our fair Miklosh pleased her. Therefore, she wanted him as a husband for her pock-marked daughter.

When the little armor-bearer went outside, the witch followed him and questioned him. "Tell me, little servant, where are you going?"

"Why shouldn't I tell! I think no good or harm will come of it. Do you see that great mountain there before us, which holds up the sky? Well,

17

we're going there. Every day, the magic queen, who is my master's sweetheart, comes to that mountain to bathe in magic milk."

"If you do as I tell you," said the witch, "you can make the magic queen love your master seven times as well as she does now. I'll give you a blow-pipe and a vase of ointment. When your master reaches the mountaintop and sits to wait for his sweetheart, take out the pipe and blow a whiff toward him. When the queen goes away, anoint his forehead with the ointment that's in the vase. Do this for three days in a row, but don't tell a living soul about it. If you do, such and such bad things will happen."

The youth, for one reason or another, took the blow-pipe and the vase and promised the witch he would do as she told him.

The blacksmith finished the twenty-four pairs of shoes and the twenty-four pairs of gloves. Miklosh and his armor-bearer took them and began to climb the unmercifully high mountain. By the time they reached the top, they'd worn out the twenty-four pairs of shoes and the twenty-four pairs of gloves, but Miklosh wasn't troubled about that.

They crossed three forests: the first of copper, the second of silver, and the third of gold. At last, they arrived at a silken meadow. In the center of the silken meadow was a golden apple tree, and under the tree was a golden tub, and in the tub was sweet fresh milk for the magic queen's bath.

Miklosh had long been striving to reach that spot, and when at last he was there, he was so tired that he lay under the apple tree to wait for the beautiful queen. While he was thinking that she was long in coming, the youth blew from the blow-pipe a light whiff of wind. In that instant, Miklosh fell into such a deep asleep that he wouldn't have woken until the day of judgment.

Just then, in the distance, thirteen swans appeared. When they reached the golden apple tree, they settled on the silken meadow, shook themselves, and became maidens.

Only then did the magic queen see her dear Miklosh. She spoke to him, but he didn't hear; she nudged him, but he didn't wake up; she kissed him, but he didn't feel her lips. At last, she cried out, "Wake up, my heart's beautiful love! Wake up from your deep sleep! Rise up from your dream, my golden one! For I can come only twice more; any more than that I can't come."

But Miklosh didn't wake up; he slept heavily. When the time came for the queen to leave, she kissed her sweetheart. The thirteen maidens shook themselves, became swans, and flew away.

The little armor-bearer rubbed Miklosh's temples with ointment he took from the vase the witch had given him.

Immediately, Miklosh sprang up, saying, "Oh, I slept well and had a beautiful dream! I dreamed the magic queen came and sat by me; that she spoke to me, but I didn't answer; that she nudged me, but I didn't wake up; that she kissed me, but I didn't feel her lips. At last, she cried out, 'Wake up, my heart's beautiful love! Wake up from your deep sleep! Rise up from your dream, my golden one! For I can come only twice more; any more than that I can't come.' Isn't it true that that was a beautiful dream?"

"It wasn't a dream, my dear master," said Yanchi, for that was the armor-bearer's name. "The magic queen was here, she spoke to you, nudged you, and kissed you, but you didn't wake up."

Miklosh was confused and sad. He couldn't explain why he hadn't woken up, but he resolved not to lie down again in case sleep overpowered him once more.

The next day, Miklosh didn't lie on the soft grass under the branches of the golden apple tree, but he walked up and down the silken meadow. Suddenly, he felt a gentle breath strike his face. His eyelids grew heavy, and his knees knocked together. He dropped to the ground, stretched out slowly on the soft grass, and fell asleep.

The thirteen swans came to the tree, shook themselves, and became maidens. The magic queen spoke to Miklosh, but he didn't hear; she shook him, but he didn't wake up; she kissed him, but he didn't feel her lips. At last, she cried out, "Wake up, my heart's beautiful love! Wake up, my heart's heart, fair Miklosh! For only once more can I come; after that, I can't come."

But Miklosh didn't wake up; he slept heavily. When the magic queen saw that in no way could she reach the soul of Miklosh, she kissed him, shook herself, became a swan, and flew away.

The armor-bearer rubbed Miklosh's temple with the ointment the blacksmith's wife had given him. Immediately, Miklosh sprang up and said, "Oh, I slept well, and I had a beautiful dream!" Then he told what he had seen.

"My dear master," said the armor-bearer, "that wasn't a dream. It really happened."

Miklosh was confused and sad, but he comforted himself with the thought that the magic queen would come once more, and this time he wouldn't sleep. But his poor head could do nothing. When the hour came, a gentle breath struck his face. His eyelids grew as heavy as stones, and his knees came together. He fell and slowly stretched out on the soft grass.

Again, the thirteen swans came to the golden apple tree, shook themselves, and became maidens. The queen went to Miklosh. She spoke to him, but he didn't answer; she pushed him, but he didn't wake up; she kissed him, but he didn't feel her lips. At last, she cried out, "Wake up, my heart's beautiful love! Wake up, fair Miklosh! I'm here for the last time!" But Miklosh didn't wake up.

When the queen saw that in no way could she reach the soul of Miklosh, she turned to the youth and said, "Tell your master that I take kind farewell of him, and that if he had hung his arms from a smaller nail onto a larger nail, he wouldn't have to wander again in a strange land."

The queen kissed Miklosh, shook herself, became a swan, and flew away, followed by the twelve other swans.

She had barely gone when the youth rubbed Miklosh's temples with the magic ointment. That moment, Miklosh sprang up, saying, "Oh, I've slept well, and I've had a beautiful dream!"

"That was no dream," said the youth. "That all happened. The magic queen came, and when she couldn't wake you up, she told me, 'Tell your master that I take a kind farewell of him, and that if he had hung his arms from a smaller onto a larger nail, he wouldn't have to wander again in a strange land.' "

Only then did the scales fall from Miklosh's eyes, only then did he understand why he had slept, only then did he know that the youth was at fault. Therefore, drawing his sword, he shouted at the servant in great anger, "You son of a beast! What did you do to me?"

"Have mercy on my head!" cried the youth. "I'm the cause of nothing. The blacksmith's wife deceived me; she gave me this little pipe and told me to blow a soft breath on you, and when the magic queen went away, to rub your temples with ointment from this vase."

Miklosh was so angry that he wouldn't have spared his own brother. He drew his sword and punished the wicked youth. Then he went down the unmercifully high mountain, and again he hung the world on his neck and gave his head to wandering.

Miklosh traveled across forty-nine kingdoms, and beyond the Operantsia Sea, and beyond the Glass Mountain, and still beyond that until he reached a broad valley in the middle of which was a king's castle. In a window of the castle, he saw a beautiful woman, and she was no other than his own sister, Tlonka, whom the dragon had carried away. They recognized each other at once.

Miklosh needed no more; he ran up the twelve marble steps, took the golden key, opened the boxwood door, and greeted his sister. Tlonka had just become the mother of a wonderful boy. As soon as he came into the world, he could talk and walk, but that wasn't strange, for he was a magic boy.[2]

"Mother," he said, "I'll free you from the dragon. I know where his strength is. Give me the key to the cellar. In the seventh niche of the cellar

---

[2] It was a popular belief that children born of a human woman and a dragon were always heroes.

is a stone jar; in the stone jar is an iron jar; in the iron jar is a copper jar; in the copper jar is a silver jar; in the silver jar is a golden jar; in the golden jar is a crystal jar; in the crystal jar is a diamond jar; and in that jar is the wine of life. If I pour it out, the dragon will lose his strength and die."

The mother found the key, the magic boy took it, and the three went to the seventh niche of the cellar. The boy, where he got it or where he didn't, took a large hammer, and saying, "Stone hoops burst; stone jar empty!" struck the jar such a blow that it fell apart. He struck the iron jar, saying, "Iron hoops burst; iron jar empty!" The iron jar fell apart. Saying, "Copper hoops burst; copper jar empty!" he struck the copper jar a hero's blow, and it fell apart. He broke the silver, golden, crystal, and diamond jars in the same way. In the diamond jar, the wine of life was seething.

Where it came from or where it didn't, the magic boy had a dipper. He took a good long drink of the wine of life, and then he gave some to his mother and uncle. What little remained, he drank himself. From this drinking, the magic boy, his mother, and Miklosh were seven times stronger than before. They closed the seventh niche of the cellar and went out under the clear sky.

The dragon was struggling home, so weak he could barely move, just as if he weren't his own self but had borrowed himself.

"Your day is finished!" said the magic boy. "You won't torment my mother any longer. You won't torture a living soul."

"Leave me my life!" begged the dragon.

"I won't destroy your life, but I'll nail you up as a spectacle," said the boy.

He pulled the dragon to the three hundred and sixty-sixth chamber of the castle and nailed him to the wall. He put one nail into the dragon's right wing, another into his left wing, and a strong one into his tail. Then the magic boy closed the great iron door, locked it seven times with the key, and fastened it with nine bolts.

The boy said to Miklosh, "Let me tell you where to find the magic queen. She's been enchanted, but if you do what I say, we can wake her up. If you don't do as I say, you'll never see the bright sun again.

"See that unmercifully high mountain that holds up the sky? The magic queen sleeps in its very center. When we're walking along inside the mountain, do nothing except step in my tracks. If you step anywhere else, the entrance will close behind us, and we'll fall under the same spell that enchants the magic queen.

"On the road we'll travel along are every kind of creeping, crawling things, snakes and toads. Be careful not to step on one of them. If one hisses, we're lost.

"In the middle of the mountain are thirteen couches. A beautiful maiden is lying on each couch. Your mind will tell you which one of the thirteen maidens is the queen. You'll kiss her three times: the first time she'll move, the second time she'll breathe, the third time she'll wake up.

"There's a cupboard in the room where the thirteen are sleeping. Open its door and take out a golden rod which you'll find there. With the rod, strike each one of the maidens saying, 'Wake up! Rise up! Dawn is coming!' They'll spring to their feet. In the same way, strike the first snake or toad you see and say to it, 'Wake up! Rise up! Come out of your snake or toad skin!' One after another will cast off their skins and take human forms. They are all magic youths and maidens who are under a spell."

The boy turned and circled around and wherever he got them, it's enough that in his arms were three hundred and sixty-six pitch-pine torches. He gave half of the torches to his uncle, and then they traveled toward the unmercifully high mountain.

When they reached the mountain, the magic boy, after searching for a certain place, struck the rocks and said, "Open before us!"

In the twinkle of an eye, the rocks opened with a crash. Miklosh and the boy went in. It was so dark in the passage that it might be bitten, but what was the ocean-great number of torches for, if not to light up the place?

The boy went ahead, and after him walked Miklosh, who strove unceasingly to step in his nephew's footprints. On every side, and almost under their feet, were snakes and toads they had to avoid. Had they stepped on any one of them, it would have hissed or made a noise.

After crawling and climbing a long distance, they came to the center of the mountain and found there a spacious chamber. In the chamber slept the thirteen maidens.

The magic boy vanished, as if the earth had swallowed him. Miklosh kissed the magic queen once, and she moved. He kissed her a second time; she began to breathe. He kissed her a third time; she opened her eyes and saw at her side none other than her sweetheart, Miklosh the fair.

Miklosh went to the cupboard, opened the door, and took out the golden rod. Then he struck each maiden three blows, saying, "Wake up! Rise up! Dawn is coming!"

The maidens wakened and sprang to their feet.

Miklosh struck the first snake that came near him, and the first toad, and said, "Wake up! Rise up! Come out of your snake and toad skin. Take your human form!"

All the snakes and toads shook themselves and became men and women.

Miklosh found himself in a wonderful palace. The magic people bathed him in milk, wiped him with a golden towel, and nimbly combed his golden hair. They dressed him in a purple robe and crowned him king of the magic people. On his right stood the magic boy, on his left the magic queen. The son of the poor man became a king, and such blessings came on his old father and mother that they couldn't have been better.

# BATCHA AND THE DRAGON

**The Story of a Shepherd Who Slept All Winter**

Once upon a time, there lived a shepherd who was called Batcha. During the summer, he pastured his flocks high up on the mountain, where he had a little hut and a sheepfold.

One day in autumn, while he was lying on the ground, idly blowing his pipes, he chanced to look down the mountain slope. There he saw a most amazing sight. A great army of snakes, hundreds and hundreds in number, was slowly crawling toward a rocky cliff not far from where he was lying.

When they reached the cliff, every serpent bit off a leaf from a plant that was growing there. They then touched the cliff with the leaves, and the rock opened. One by one, they crawled inside. When the last one had disappeared, the rock closed.

Batcha blinked in bewilderment.

"What can this mean?" he asked himself. "Where have they gone? I think I'll have to climb up there myself and see what that plant is. I wonder if the rock will open for me."

He whistled to Dunay, his dog, and left him in charge of the sheep. Then he made his way over to the cliff and examined the mysterious plant. It was something he had never seen before.

He picked a leaf and touched the cliff in the same place where the serpents had touched it. Instantly the rock opened.

Batcha stepped inside. He found himself in a huge cavern, the walls of which glittered with gold and silver and precious stones. A golden table stood in the center and upon it a monster serpent, a very king of serpents, lay coiled up fast asleep. The other serpents, hundreds and hundreds of them, lay on the ground around the table. They also were fast asleep. As Batcha walked about, not one of them stirred.

Batcha sauntered here and there examining the walls and the golden table and the sleeping serpents. When he had seen everything, he thought to himself, "It's quite strange and interesting and all that, but now it's time for me to get back to my sheep."

25

It's easy to say "Now I'm going," but when Batcha tried to leave, he discovered he couldn't, because the rock had closed. There he was, locked in with the serpents.

He was a philosophical fellow and so, after puzzling a moment, he shrugged and said, "Well, if I can't get out, I suppose I'll have to stay here for the night."

With that, he drew his cape about himself, lay down, and was soon fast asleep.

He was awakened by a rustling murmur. Thinking he was in his own hut, he sat up and rubbed his eyes. Then he saw the glittering walls of the cavern and remembered his adventure.

The old king serpent still lay on the golden table but was no longer asleep. A movement like a slow wave was rippling his great coils. All the other serpents on the ground were facing the golden table and with darting tongues were hissing, "Is it time? Is it time?"

The old king serpent slowly lifted his head and with a deep murmurous hiss said, "Yes, it's time."

He stretched out his long body, slipped off the golden table, and glided away to the cavern wall. All the smaller serpents wriggled after him.

Batcha followed, thinking to himself, "I'll go out the way they go."

The old king serpent touched the wall with his tongue, and the rock opened. Then he glided aside, and the serpents crawled out, one by one. When the last one was out, Batcha tried to follow, but the rock swung shut in his face, locking him in again.

The old king serpent hissed at him in a deep breathy voice, "Hah, you miserable man creature, you can't get out! You're here, and here you'll stay!"

"But I can't stay here," Batcha said. "What can I do in here? I can't sleep forever! You must let me out! I have sheep at pasture and a scolding wife at home in the valley. She'll have a thing or two to say if I'm late getting back!"

Batcha pleaded and argued until at last the old serpent said, "Very well, I'll let you out, but not until you've made me a triple oath that you won't tell anyone how you came in."

Batcha agreed to this. Three times he swore a mighty oath not to tell anyone how he had entered the cavern.

"I warn you," the old serpent said, as he opened the wall, "if you break this oath, a terrible fate will overtake you!"

Without another word, Batcha hurried through the opening.

Once outside, he looked around him in surprise.

Everything seemed changed. It was autumn when he'd followed the serpents into the cavern. Now it was spring!

"What's happened?" he cried in fright. "Oh, what an unfortunate fellow I am! Have I slept through the winter? Where are my sheep? And my wife—what will she say?"

With trembling knees, he made his way to his hut. His wife was busy inside. He could see her through the open door. He didn't know what to say to her at first, so he slipped into the sheepfold and hid himself while he tried to think out some likely story.

While he was crouching there, he saw a finely dressed gentleman come to the door of the hut and ask his wife where her husband was.

The woman burst into tears and explained to the stranger that one day in the previous autumn her husband had taken out his sheep as usual and had never returned.

"Dunay, the dog," she said, "drove home the sheep, and from that day to this, nothing has ever been heard of my poor husband. I suppose a wolf devoured him, or the witches caught him and tore him into pieces and scattered him over the mountain. And here I am left, a poor forsaken widow! Oh dear, oh dear, oh dear!"

Her grief was so great that Batcha leaped out of the sheepfold to comfort her.

"There, there, dear wife, don't cry! Here I am, alive and well! No wolf ate me; no witches caught me. I've been asleep in the sheepfold—that's all. I must have slept all winter long!"

At the sight and sound of her husband, the woman stopped crying. Her grief changed to surprise, then to fury.

"You wretch!" she cried. "You lazy, good-for-nothing loafer! A nice kind of shepherd you are to desert your sheep and yourself to idle away the winter sleeping like a serpent! That's a fine story, isn't it? I suppose you think me fool enough to believe it! Oh, you—you sheep's tick, where have you been and what have you been doing?"

She flew at Batcha with both hands. There's no telling what she would have done to him if the stranger hadn't interfered.

"There, there," he said, "no use getting excited! Of course, he hasn't been sleeping here in the sheepfold all winter. The question is, where has he been? Here's some money for you. Take it and go along home to your cottage in the valley. Leave Batcha to me, and I promise you I'll get the truth out of him."

The woman abused her husband some more and then, pocketing the money, went off.

As soon as she was gone, the stranger changed into a horrible looking creature with a third eye in the middle of his forehead.

"Good heavens!" Batcha gasped in fright. "He's the wizard of the mountain! Now what's going to happen to me!"

Batcha had often heard terrifying stories of the wizard, how he could himself take any form he wished, and how he could turn a man into a ram.

"Aha!" The wizard laughed. "I see you know me! Now then, no more lies! Tell me where you've been all winter long."

At first, Batcha remembered his triple oath to the old king serpent, and he feared to break it. But when the wizard thundered out the same question a second time and a third time, and grew bigger and more horrible looking each time he spoke, Batcha forgot his oath and confessed everything.

"Now come with me," the wizard said. "Show me the cliff. Show me the magic plant."

What could Batcha do but obey? He led the wizard to the cliff and picked a leaf of the magic plant.

"Open the rock," the wizard commanded.

Batcha laid the leaf against the cliff, and instantly the rock opened.

"Go inside!" the wizard ordered.

But Batcha's trembling legs refused to move.

The wizard took out a book and began mumbling an incantation. Suddenly, the earth trembled, the sky thundered, and with a great hissing, whistling sound, a monster dragon flew out of the cavern. It was the old king serpent whose seven years were up and who had now become a flying dragon. From his huge mouth, he breathed out fire and smoke. With his long tail, he swished right and left among the forest trees, and these snapped and broke like little twigs.

The wizard, still mumbling from his book, handed Batcha a bridle.

"Throw this around his neck!" he commanded.

Batcha took the bridle but was too terrified to act. The wizard spoke again, and Batcha made one uncertain step in the dragon's direction and lifted his arm to throw the bridle over the dragon's head. The dragon suddenly turned and swooped under Batcha. Before he knew what was happening, Batcha found himself on the dragon's back, being lifted up, up, up, above the tops of the forest trees, above the very mountains themselves.

For a moment, the sky was so dark that only the fire, spurting from the dragon's eyes and mouth, lighted them on their way.

The dragon lashed this way and that in fury, he belched forth great floods of boiling water, he hissed, he roared, until Batcha, clinging to his back, was half dead with fright.

Gradually, the dragon's anger cooled. He ceased belching forth boiling water, he stopped breathing fire, and his hisses grew less terrifying.

"Thank God!" Batcha gasped. "Perhaps now he'll sink to earth and let me go."

But the dragon wasn't yet finished with punishing Batcha for breaking his oath. He rose still higher until the mountains of the earth looked like tiny ant hills, still up until even these had disappeared. On, on they went, whizzing through the stars of heaven.

At last, the dragon stopped flying and hung motionless in the firmament. To Batcha, this was even more terrifying than moving.

"What can I do? What can I do?" he wept in agony. "If I jump down to earth, I'll kill myself, and I can't fly on up to heaven! Oh, dragon, have mercy on me! Fly back to earth and let me go, and I swear before God that never again until death will I offend you!"

Batcha's pleading would have moved a stone to pity, but the dragon, with an angry shake of his tail, only hardened his heart.

Suddenly, Batcha heard the sweet voice of the sky lark that was mounting to heaven.

"Sky lark!" he called. "Dear sky lark, bird that God loves, help me, for I'm in great trouble! Fly up to heaven and tell God Almighty that Batcha, the shepherd, is hung in midair on a dragon's back. Tell Him that Batcha praises Him forever and begs Him to deliver him."

The sky lark carried this message to heaven. God Almighty, pitying the poor shepherd, took some birch leaves and wrote on them in letters of gold. He put them in the sky lark's bill and told the sky lark to drop them on the dragon's head.

The sky lark returned from heaven and, hovering over Batcha, dropped the birch leaves on the dragon's head.

The dragon instantly sank to earth, so fast that Batcha lost consciousness.

When he came to himself, he was sitting before his own hut. He looked around him. The dragon's cliff had disappeared. Otherwise, everything was the same.

It was late afternoon, and Dunay, the dog, was driving home the sheep. There was a woman, Batcha's wife, coming up the mountain path.

Batcha heaved a great sigh.

"Thank God I'm back!" he said to himself. "How fine it is to hear Dunay's bark! And here comes my wife, God bless her! She'll scold me, I know, but even if she does, how glad I am to see her!"

# THE LAUGHING APPLES AND
# THE WEEPING QUINCES

Once upon a time, there was a king who had an only son, and the king wished greatly that this son should marry as soon as possible. The more the king urged his son to find a wife, the more the young man showed his distaste for marriage, saying that women were good for nothing, that they were in the world for the purpose of deceiving men. When the king saw that his words were useless, he led his son into a large hall, where portraits of women were hung along the walls.

The king said, "Here, my son, are the portraits of all the unmarried princesses in the world. Look at them and make your choice."

The young man, to gratify his father, examined one portrait after another, but was pleased with none. One was too young, another too old, one too pale, another too red, and so he went on until he came to a portrait that was hung with the face to the wall.

He said, "Tell me, dear father, why is this portrait hung with the face to the wall?"

"Leave it as it is," answered the king. "It represents a beautiful maiden, but she's as adverse to marriage as you are. She's ruined every prince who's asked her for her hand."

To this, the prince answered, "You brought me here to see all the princesses there are in the world; you have no right to withhold one of them." With these words, he turned the portrait around and examined it more carefully than he had the others.

The maiden it represented was so beautiful she won his heart, and he said to his father, "This one or none."

The old king did what he could to dissuade his son. He explained that the maiden's father was a powerful king, that by the tasks she had set, she had ruined the most renowned princes in the world, that if he asked for her in marriage, he would lose his life. "Moreover," the king said, "have pity on me; don't make me a victim of misery in my final days."

But his words were useless. The prince clung to his resolution, but he said he would go in disguise and not as an open wooer. When he had gained his father's permission, he put on coarse garments, gave himself as poor an appearance as possible, and set out for the city in which the princess lived.

The road led through a wide, barren field. There he saw two men struggling desperately with each other. He went up to them and asked, "Why are you fighting so fiercely? Can I settle your dispute?"

They repulsed him with rude speech and told him not to get mixed up in their affairs, but to go on his way.

The prince was not to be put off. He said, "Tell me what you're fighting about, and I'll give you its value in money. Then you'll have peace."

At that, one of them said, "See here, you fool, these are the inheritances our father left us. It's these we're fighting about." He showed the prince a rugged staff and an old cap that lay on the ground nearby.

When the prince saw the staff and the cap, he laughed heartily and said, "You ought to be ashamed to fight over such trifles. Tell me what they're worth. I'll give one of you the money; the other can take the cap and staff, and you'll both be happy."

"You can settle the price yourself," replied the man, "but only when you know the power of these things. Whoever puts on the cap becomes invisible; whoever strikes three times with the staff is borne wherever he wishes."

"I don't have enough money to pay for such articles," said the prince, "but I can settle your dispute. I'll hurl a dart at that tree over there. The two of you must run for the dart; the one who returns it to me will have the staff and the cap."

They agreed to this. The prince hurled his dart at the tree, and both men rushed after it. While they were running, the prince put the cap on his head, struck the earth three times with the staff, and wished himself in the palace of the princess.

Scarcely had he uttered the wish when he was there. He went from room to room until he came to where the princess was. When he saw her, he thought she was more beautiful than her portrait. He gazed at her for a while, then went to the garden and asked for the head-gardener. When he found him, he offered himself as an assistant and was told that only strong-fisted workmen were needed, that no use could be made of white-handed fools. But when he said that he asked no wages, his food would be sufficient reward, the head-gardener hired him.

The prince worked in the garden one day after another, keeping near the favorite resort of the princess, in order to be able to look at her. She loved the garden, and every afternoon she came there and walked around for a while. Afterward, she went to a secluded summer-house and read until late into the night. No one knew at what hour she returned to the palace. The prince thought he would find out, so he made a hiding place. When night came and the other workmen had gone to bed, he crept into the place and watched.

At last, toward midnight, he heard a rolling noise, like distant thunder; it came nearer and nearer. The princess came out of the summer-house. At that moment, a tremendous dragon flew up and dropped to the ground in front of her. She welcomed him and led him into the summer-house. The prince saw how friendly she was, but he was too far away to hear her words. He wanted to go nearer, but he was afraid of the dragon.

After a time, the dragon flew away, with the same thundering and the same lightning speed with which he came, and the princess hurried into the palace.

The prince went to his room, but thoughts of the dragon drove sleep from his eyes. The next day, he remembered his staff and cap. When night came, he put on the cap, took the staff in his hand, and went to the summer-house and waited for the dragon. The princess received the dragon as kindly as before, and he began to urge her to go to his castle where a grand banquet was awaiting her. At first, she refused, saying her father had appointed an early hour in the morning for an interview; that the castle was six hundred days' journey away; and she might not return in time. But when the dragon promised to bring her back before daybreak, she consented. He took her in his claws and flew away.

The prince struck the earth three times with his staff, wished himself at the dragon's castle, and was there at the same time as the dragon and the princess.

The castle was surrounded with high walls and was inhabited by a host of serving dragons. The halls, lighted by thousands of lamps, were gleaming in splendor. In the last one, which was the most beautiful of all, a banquet was spread.

The dragon gave the princess a napkin embroidered with such marvelous skill that she wouldn't use it, but hung it on a nail, saying, "I'll take this napkin home; it's too beautiful to use."

When the princess sat at the feast, the prince took the napkin from the nail and put it inside his shirt. Then he sat at the table and ate of every dish that was brought. When a dish of rice was served, the dragon saw that near the holes made by his spoon and that of the princess sitting opposite, a third one appeared. He pointed this out to the princess and asked her how it happened. While she was wondering, the dragon turned the dish around to see if their eyes had deceived them, and, behold, a fourth hole was made, and it grew larger every minute.

Not understanding how this could be, the princess grew restless and uneasy and urged the dragon to take her home. When she rose from the table and turned to get the napkin, she saw that it wasn't there. That alarmed her even more, and she urged the dragon to hurry. He took her in his claws and bore her home as swiftly as he had borne her to the castle. The prince kept pace with them and saw how the princess hurried into her father's palace.

The next morning when the prince went to the garden, he saw by the restless running to and fro of people that something had happened. When he met the head-gardener, he ventured to ask the cause of the disturbance.

"We're lost beyond redemption," answered the gardener. "A neighboring king, whose army is four times as large as ours, has sent ambassadors to demand our princess in marriage for his son. He says that if the suit is not granted, he'll declare war against our king and so ravage his kingdom that not one stone will be left upon another. This morning the princess gave her answer. She declared she'd give her hand only to the man who could solve three problems for her, that such had been her terms up until now, and such they would remain. If the prince wished to marry her, let him make his venture. When the ambassadors heard this, they declared war in the name of their king and departed in haste. And now our king can't find a commander-in-chief who dares to march against such an enemy."

"I'll be commander-in-chief," said the prince. "Go to the king and tell him that if he makes me commander-in-chief, I vow not only to conquer the enemy, but to take half of his kingdom."

When the gardener heard these words, he couldn't believe his ears and cried out again and again, "The fellow has lost his wits! You poor devil, do you mean to say that you have the impudence to offer yourself as commander-in-chief? I won't go to the king, but to the marshal of the palace and ask him to lock you up, so you don't come to harm with your madness."

The prince repeated his request with such insistence and had such a noble, resolute bearing, that by degrees he made an impression on the gardener, who at last said, "I know they'll lock us both up, but since you've asked me to do this, I'll undertake it. I won't go to the king, but to the chancellor and tell him what you said."

When the chancellor heard the message the head gardener brought, he laughed loudly and said, "Fright has made you gardeners crazy. I must lock you up. But I'll look at the fellow first. Bring him here."

When the prince appeared before the chancellor, the prince's bearing made such an impression on the chancellor that he rose and, shaking his head, went to the king and laid before him the gardener's astonishing proposal.

At first, the king laughed, but when it was explained to him that the kingdom could be saved only by a miracle, he became thoughtful and asked to have the gardener summoned. The dignity of the prince and his words inspired the king with confidence. He grasped him by the hand, presented him to his warriors as their commander-in-chief, and said, "You must march at once, because our enemy has already crossed the border."

The prince went forward with fifty thousand men and camped in front of the enemy. When they saw the small number of his men, his opponents sent a herald demanding surrender to avoid bloodshed. The prince answered that the following day would show whose blood would be shed.

The generals waited on the prince, asking for his plan for the battle, but the prince didn't tell them anything. When night came, the prince lay down to rest. He rose at midnight, put on his cap, and, taking his staff, wished to be in the enemy's camp. He slipped into the tents where commanders and officers were sleeping and cut off their heads. He worked until nearly morning, then wished himself back in his own tent.

When day came, the enemy found a huge number of their leaders dead. They called together the sentinels, who swore in one voice that no one had gone either into or out of the camp. The regiments that had lost their leaders began to cry out treason, saying this explained the unexampled boldness of the enemy. Those suspected of treason gathered to defend themselves against the unjust charge. There could be no thought of battle that day.

The following night, the prince went again to the enemy's camp, and, if possible, killed a greater number of leaders than before.

The next morning the cry of treason was twice as great. Words became deeds, and soon the enemy's legions were fighting with one another.

When the prince heard the uproar, he cried out, "Now is the time to strike!"

He rushed forward with his army and slaughtered so many of his foes that few escaped. Then he marched to the capital and forced the enemy king to a peace by which he gave up half of his kingdom. When the prince, at the head of his victorious army, returned home, the good king received him with great honor and made him chancellor of the kingdom. The prince filled the office with such wisdom and prudence that he rose daily in the king's esteem.

After a certain time, the prince went to the king and declared that he couldn't remain in his service; he must return to his own country. The king was alarmed; he explained to the prince the danger the kingdom would be in if he left, because it was only fear of the prince that kept the enemy from taking vengeance for his overthrow. The king implored the prince to remain and declared that he would grant his every wish, as long as it was within his power.

The prince withstood the king's entreaties until the king became greatly embarrassed and troubled, then the prince said he loved the king's daughter and would remain if she'd become his wife. When the king heard this, he said, "I'd gladly make you my son-in-law, but you know the stubbornness of my daughter. I'm afraid she'll treat you as she has other men who've wished to marry her."

The king sent for his daughter, told her of the chancellor's desire, and commanded her to accept the proposal.

Upon hearing her father's words, the princess was beside herself with anger and cried out, "Has it come to this, that I, who have refused the most mighty princes, must marry a gardener?"

She used every means to change her father's mind, but her prayers were of no avail this time. The king wouldn't be influenced.

When she saw this, she said, "I'll yield to your wishes only on one condition—that this gardener perform three tasks. I'll think them over and give him the first one tomorrow morning." She left her father, without listening to what he might say.

That evening, the prince put on his cap and, taking the staff in his hand, went to the summer-house to wait for the dragon's arrival.

When the beast came, the princess met him and said, "I have another wooer, no other than our new chancellor, the ex-gardener."

When the dragon heard this, he laughed until the house trembled.

"Don't take it so lightly," said the princess. "There's something mysterious about the man. I've long suspected him of being intimate with magic. Think hard before you tell me what task to give him."

Then the dragon answered, "Tell him to bring you, within twenty-four hours, three laughing apples. The only tree upon which such apples grow is in my garden, six hundred days' journey from here, and a hundred dragons guard the tree."

When the dragon flew back to his castle, the prince followed him and saw how he posted his servants around the tree and charged them to watch it the entire night, so that not even a bird could approach it. When the sentinels had taken their places, the prince went to the tree and broke off a branch which held ten apples. As soon as he touched the branch, all the apples on the tree began to laugh, "Ha! Ha! Ha! Ha!" The dragons sprang up, fell over each other, and crowded together. They knew someone had touched the apples, but search as they might, they couldn't find anyone.

The next morning, when the princess gave the chancellor his task, he declared that he was ready to accomplish it. To the astonishment of the king and his whole court, the prince transacted his business all day without taking the least trouble about the task. Toward evening, he put the ten apples on a plate and gave them to the king. When the princess saw the apples, she wondered greatly if they were the laughing apples, because they looked like common apples. The prince told her to touch them. When she did, the hall rang with loud laughter, and she was obliged to confess that he had accomplished the first task.

That evening, the prince listened to the conversation between the princess and the dragon. The dragon told her she must ask the chancellor to bring her three weeping quinces, that the only tree on which such quinces grew stood in the court of his castle. He would close the door of the court and place sentinels around the tree.

It happened with the weeping quinces as with the laughing apples.

The prince, wearing his cap of invisibility, followed the dragon to his castle. When the dragon had posted his sentinels, he himself sat near the tree. Then the prince broke off a branch with three quinces on it. That instant, all the quinces on the tree began to weep. The dragon and sentinels rushed around in search of the thief. They looked in every nook and crevice, but found no one.

The prince amused himself a while with the mad racing around of the dragons, then wished himself back in the king's garden. The next day, he placed the quinces on a dish, as he had the apples. When the princess touched them, they began to weep. She saw with alarm that he had fulfilled the second task.

That night, the dragon was extra thoughtful. At last, he said to the princess, "This task will surely bring the gardener to destruction. Tell him to get you a tooth from the jaw of the dragon, to whom the tree with the laughing apples and the tree with the weeping quinces belong. If he tries to tear out one of my teeth, I'll swallow him alive."

When the prince heard this, he wished himself in the tool house. There he got pincers and a basket, and, taking sleep-inducing herbs, returned to the summer-house and followed the dragon to his castle.

There, the dragon collected forty of his strongest attendants and commanded them to watch the entire night through. The prince placed the herbs on each one of the dragons, and soon they were all asleep, snoring, with jaws wide open.

The prince drew a front tooth from the jaw of each dragon, put the teeth into his basket, and was back in the king's garden.

When the dragons woke up, one dragon saw a cavity in the jaw of another and exclaimed, "Oh, my friend, you've lost a front tooth!"

When each dragon discovered that he had lost a front tooth, great fear seized them all. "He who has pulled out our teeth can cut our throats!"

The prince displayed the teeth as he had the apples and the quinces. When he exhibited them before the princess, she fainted from terror.

That night when he went to the summer-house, he found the princess waiting for the dragon. She waited a long time. When the dragon eventually came, he looked around anxiously and said to the princess, "Your suitor has accomplished the third task. He who can pull out my teeth can cut my throat or take your life. You'll never see me again." And he flew away.

The next morning the prince, taking his cap and staff, went to the palace. He found the entire court assembled, and the princess in a bridal dress. She looked at him kindly, but he passed her. Standing before the king, he asked for a private audience. When they were alone, he told the king who he was and related the whole story. He told the king that his daughter had been enchanted by a dragon, that now the spell was broken, and the dragon had fled. Then he bade the king farewell, struck the floor three times with his staff, and disappeared.

Back to his father's palace he went. When he greeted his father, he said, "Here I am, cured of my love, and ready to marry the woman you'll give me!"

His father made a great feast and hastened to find a beautiful wife for his son. When the king was dying, a host of grandchildren stood around his bed.

# IVAN POPYALOF

O nce upon a time, there lived an old couple who had three sons. Two of these were bright lads, but the third one, named Ivan, was not as smart. He lay among the stove ashes for twelve years. In doing so, he gained the name of Popyalof, which means ashes. One day, he arose and shook himself, so that more than 200 pounds of ash fell off him.

In the land where Ivan lived, it was always as dark as night. That was a dragon's doing, because the creature had swallowed the sun. Ivan decided to kill that dragon, so the light would return. He said, "Father, make me a 200-pound mace."

Ivan may not have been as intelligent as his brothers (or so they thought), but he was quite strong. When he received the mace, he went out into a field, flung the weapon straight up into the sky, and then left to go home. The next day, he returned to the spot where he had hurled the mace. He waited a long time, with his head thrown back, watching, waiting. At long last, the mace hurtled downward and hit him on the forehead. Ivan remained unharmed, but the mace broke in two.

Ivan set off for home. When he arrived, he said, "Father, make me another mace, a 400-pound one this time."

As soon as the new mace was finished, Ivan returned to the field and flung the mace skyward. It flew higher and higher. For three days and three nights, it soared through the sky. On the fourth day, Ivan returned to the same spot and waited. The mace soon tumbled down, and Ivan put his knee into its path. The mace broke into three pieces, but once again, Ivan suffered no injury.

The boy returned home and told his father to make him yet another mace, one that weighed 600 pounds. For a third time, Ivan went to the field and tossed the mace upward. It sailed through the sky for six days. On the seventh, Ivan waited in the same spot as before. Down fell the mace. Faster and faster, it sped toward him. When it struck Ivan, it bent his forehead under the force.

At this, Ivan said, "This mace will do for the dragon!"

He prepared for his journey. When everything was ready, he traveled with his brothers to fight the dragon. They rode and rode for miles, for days, for so long they lost track of how long they'd been gone. Deep in the woods, they eventually saw a hut that stood on slender supports, or some who tell the tale, say it was chicken legs.

The brothers had arrived at the dragon's home!

All the party stood still. What should they do now?

Ivan came out of his stupor and pulled off his gloves, hung them on a fence, and said to his brothers, "If blood starts to drip from my gloves, hurry to help me."

After giving his command, he went into the hut and huddled beneath the raised floor that served as the dragon's bed.

In no time at all, a three-headed dragon rode up on his horse, accompanied by his hounds and falcon. The horse stumbled, the hounds howled, and his falcon screeched.

The dragon shouted, "What's the matter? Why did you stumble, horse? And howl, hounds? And screech, falcon?"

"How can I help but stumble?" replied the horse. "Ivan Popyalof is sitting in the house under the floorboards."

Then the dragon said, "Come outside, Ivan! Let's see who's stronger."

Ivan left the hut and fought the dragon. With ease, Ivan killed the dragon, and then he sat beneath the floorboards again.

Soon, a six-headed dragon returned to the hut. Once again, the beast challenged Ivan to fight. Ivan killed that one, too.

Finally, a third dragon returned home. This one was more fearsome than the others, because he had twelve heads. This didn't terrify Ivan. He fought the beast and chopped off nine of his heads. Ivan was tired, and the dragon was also nearing the end of his strength.

Just then, a raven flew by and croaked, "*Krof? Krof!* Blood? Blood! Who should I help?"

The dragon cried to the raven, "Fly away! Tell my wife to come and devour Ivan Popyalof, and I'll give you gold."

But Ivan cried, "Fly away! Tell my brothers to come help me. When we kill this dragon, we'll give you his flesh to eat."

The raven listened to Ivan, flew to his brothers, and began to croak above their heads. When the brothers heard the raven's cry, they awoke and hurried to Ivan's aid. The three of them killed the dragon, took his heads into the cabin, and destroyed them in the fireplace.

Immediately, bright light shone again throughout the entire land.

After killing the dragon, Ivan Popyalof and his brothers set off toward home, but Ivan had forgotten to retrieve his gloves. He told his brothers to wait for him while he went back to fetch his gloves. When he arrived at the hut and was reaching for his gloves, he heard the voices of the dragon's wife and daughters talking inside the hut.

Curious what was happening, Ivan turned himself into a cat and mewled outside the door. The dragonesses let him in, and he listened to everything they said. And like a cat, he soon decided that inside was not where he wanted to be, so he scratched at the door until they let him out again. He returned to a human, grabbed his gloves, and hurried away.

As soon as he came to where his brothers were, he mounted his horse, and they all started out again. They rode and rode. Soon, they came to a green meadow, and on that meadow lay silk cushions.

The oldest brother said, "I'm exhausted. Let's allow our horses to graze here while we rest a bit."

But Ivan said, "Wait a minute, brothers!"

Ivan seized his mace and struck the cushions. Blood streamed out, staining the cushions red.

The brothers hurried away from the ghastly sight. They rode and rode. Soon, they approached a tree, loaded with gold and silver apples.

The second oldest brother said, "I'm starving. Let's eat some apples."

But Ivan said, "Wait a minute, brothers. I'll try them first."

He grasped his mace and struck the apple tree with it. Blood streamed out, soaking the trunk and ground.

Again, the brothers scurried away from the terrible place. They rode and rode. Finally, they reached a spring.

The oldest brother cried, "Let's stop and have a drink of water."

"Surely, the spring is safe to drink from," added the second brother.

But Ivan Popyalof cried, "Stop, brothers!"

He raised his mace and struck the spring. Its water turned bright red with blood.

"How is this possible?" Ivan's brothers asked.

"The silk cushions, the apple tree, and the spring were the daughters of the twelve-headed dragon," Ivan replied. "They planned to kill us by trickery."

After killing the dragon's daughters, Ivan and his brothers continued their homeward journey. Soon, the dragon's wife flew after them. She landed on the path in front of Ivan and opened her jaws, which reached from the sky to the earth, in order to swallow him. But Ivan and his brothers threw 100 pounds of salt into her mouth. She swallowed the salt and flew away, thinking it was Ivan Popyalof.

She suffered a terrible thirst and drank from a lake until satisfied. Realizing she'd been tricked and had eaten salt and not Ivan, she again flew after him.

Sensing more danger, Ivan hurried toward a village. He and his brothers hid behind twelve doors in the forge belonging to Kuzma and Demian, those saintly, supernatural smiths who took upon themselves the task of battling dragons.

The dragon's wife flew up as Ivan shut the last door behind him. She said, "Give me Ivan Popyalof."

One of the smiths replied, "You'll have to get him yourself. Stick your tongue through all twelve doors and take him."

The dragon's wife began licking the doors, twisting her tongue through one keyhole after the other.

Meanwhile the smiths heated iron tongs. As soon as the dragon's wife slipped her tongue through into the smithy, the men held her appendage tight and beat her with hammers. When she died, they burned her body and scattered the ashes into the wind.

The brothers returned home. There, they lived and enjoyed themselves, feasting and partying, and drinking beer and wine.

*I was there too and had liquor to drink. It didn't go into my mouth, but only ran down my beard.*

# The Emperor of the Fish

*Once upon a time, if it hadn't happened, it wouldn't have been talked about, and the story would've ended here.*

There once was a man, who fished for a living; this man had a son, and he taught him his craft, because he didn't know anything else.

One day, while using his net, he caught a great, beautiful fish; its scales shone bright like diamonds. After the man caught it, he took it to the shore and gave it to his son to hold. The son brought the fish to the pond, to try to catch it once again.

As soon as the fisherman went away, the son heard the fish talking with a soft voice, as though crying, "You, little boy, little boy, throw me back into the water, because I'm the Emperor of the fish. If you do me good, I'll do you good, as well."

The boy was in awe when he heard the fish talking, and because he felt sorry for it, for its begging that could soften a heart made of coal, he threw it into the pond.

The fish, seeing itself in its environment, dived deep once and returned to the surface, then it dived deep into the water for good.

A while had passed and the fisherman returned, swearing like a mad man, because he hadn't caught any other fish. "At least we have the other fish," he said.

"I threw it into the water, dad, because it spoke and begged me to let it go. It said it was the Emperor of the fish," responded the boy.

The fisherman didn't wait to try to catch anything else. Since he was sad, he started beating the boy. The fisherman hit the boy and kept hitting him until the fisherman got tired and let the boy go.

They went home, and that evening they really fasted. They fasted even more than they did on Easter's Eve, because they had literally nothing to eat.

The second day, the fisherman started to beat the boy again, today, tomorrow, and so on, until at one point, the boy couldn't stand the beatings anymore, and he left.

He went straight ahead for a long time and reached a city. As soon as he entered it, a dwarf appeared near a wall and greeted him. Being alone, the boy gladly made friends with the dwarf and became blood brothers, swearing never to part and whatever they had, to share in half. They swore to share, but what could they share? Both being broke, they decided to become servants.

They found a place with the same master; they got hired, and it was done. One day, while lying near the gate, because his errands were finished, the dwarf saw a man mounted on a horse, and this man was leading five other horses and had a servant, too. The next day, at around the same time, the man with the horses passed again with another servant, the third day again, and every single day he passed by with different servants.

The dwarf, seeing that he was always changing his servants, thought, "I wonder what he's doing with the old servants." But he couldn't figure it out. One day, he decided to follow the man, to see where he went and what he did.

He left for the market; there he waited for the rich man to pass by. The rich man saw a guy doing nothing, so he hired him, mounted him on his horse, and left together. The dwarf followed them. They passed through a beautiful garden, full of flowers; then they entered a forest and walked for a while, until they stopped at the roots of a great tree. When they stopped, they got off the horse, and the rich man took a rope out of his bag, hung it in a hook, hammered it onto the tree, and the servant climbed up.

The man climbed up to the top of the tree, and guess what he saw?

Believe it or not, it was a huge basket full of gemstones.

"Oh my God, my lord, they almost blinded me, all these gems!" said the servant from the tree.

"Come on and bring it down," said the rich man, "and stop yelling from there."

The servant took the basket down. The rich man emptied it into bags and then gave the servant the basket to put back into the tree.

The servant climbed back up, put the basket back, and when he wanted to come down, there was no rope anymore!

"Hang the rope back, my lord, so I can get down. I can't jump from here. I'll break a bone and become a cripple."

The rich man placed his bags on the horses without answering.

"Hey, can't you hear me? Stop fooling around," said the servant.

He kept talking, but the rich man ignored him and mounted on his horse, leaving.

"Hey, lord, hey, wait, wait. Hey, come back and help me get down. We didn't agree to leave me here."

The lord kept running, like running for his life.

The poor servant, seeing that it wasn't a joke anymore and the lord had gone, started crying in the most lamentable way.

The dwarf stayed hidden, because he wanted to see what happened next.

While the servant kept yelling, suddenly, a dragon, with a frightening mouth, appeared from a burrow of the tree and started climbing upward. When it reached the top, where the poor man was sitting, it opened its great mouth, with its teeth the size of a shovel and swallowed the man whole. After it swallowed him, it spit gemstones back into the basket—some were red, green, others were white—until the basket was full, then it climbed down and went back to its burrow.

The poor dwarf was petrified with fear, and he felt sorry for the poor Romanian, but when he saw the dragon going back into its burrow, he turned around and went back home.

The second day, when the rich man passed with his wagon through the market, guess who offered to help him in the woods? The poor dwarf, him indeed! Who knew what he had in mind?

The two bartered, and off he went. He passed with the rich man through the town, through the garden, and through the forest until they reached the said tree. As soon as they arrived, the rich man hung the rope, and the dwarf climbed up, took the basket as he was told, and then climbed back down.

After the rich man emptied the gemstones into his bags, he gave the dwarf the basket and told him to put it back. The dwarf refused, claiming to be dizzy.

How could he climb up? If he climbed, he would have to climb down, because he wasn't crazy to stay there, and if he climbed down, and nobody was left in the tree, the serpent wouldn't leave other gemstones.

"Climb up, man! I'll even give you a handful of those gemstones."

The dwarf turned him down.

"Climb up. That was our deal."

"Aww! My good lord, everything is spinning around me," shouted the dwarf, while rolling on the ground and ignoring the lord's words.

Seeing there was no other way, the lord took the basket and climbed up to put it back.

That's what the dwarf expected. As soon as he saw the man up in the tree, nothing was spinning around him anymore. He took the rope out of the hook and left the rich man hanging in the tree.

"Don't touch the rope! What are you doing? Let me climb down!"

"I think you're exactly where you need to be," said the dwarf.

"Hey, dwarf, I'll give you bags full of gemstones! You only have to hang the rope back, so I can climb down."

The dwarf kept refusing. After he finished his work, he mounted the horse and left while saying, "Farewell, my perched cousin," and went back into the town.

The poor rich lord tried to go up, tried to move down, nothing worked! If he jumped, he would split his head open, and that would be it for him. He started crying and crying, until the dragon heard him! The great serpent climbed up, ate the lord—and this is how the rich man met his end.

Now what the dwarf wanted was to find the lord's house, but he didn't know where to start looking for it. He let the horses go wherever they wanted, and they led him straight to the lord's home. There, the dwarf found the gates locked, but he located the keys in the lord's bags, opened the gates, and went inside. He'd never seen more wealth in his entire life, but he came back to his senses, emptied the bags, and left to find his friend.

The poor fisherman boy was sad—he didn't know where the dwarf was. The moment the boy saw the dwarf, his eyes lit up with joy.

"What have you done? Where have you been?" he kept asking.

"Don't worry. I'll tell you everything eventually," said the dwarf. "Now take your bag and come with me."

The boy listened, went to his master, told him he was leaving and needed what he had earned.

"Are you crazy, man, or what? How come you're suddenly leaving me?"

"You have to give me what's mine," said the boy. "I'm not staying here anymore."

"He's a mad one," thought the master. "I'd better give him what he wants and get him off my mind; you never know what he could do next."

He gave the boy what he had earned. "Here, now. God's speed, boy."

The boy left, and the dwarf took him to the rich man's house. Upon entering the house, the boy froze in awe, when the dwarf told him that all that wealth was theirs.

"My friend, have pity on my soul!"

"I swear to God!"

"All this wealth is ours?"

"Yes, indeed."

"You did great, my friend!" he finally said, after he heard the dwarf's story.

Because the fisherman's son and the dwarf got royally rich overnight, everybody heard about them. At that time, the Emperor had a daughter he wanted to marry and told the entire world that whoever managed to stay for an entire night in the same room with her would be her husband. This girl was married ninety-nine times before, but every single groom died and only their bones were found the following day. Nobody knew who ate them.

Hearing that, the dwarf wasted no more time and went to the Emperor's palace to tell him that he had a sworn brother, who would try to marry the girl.

The Emperor accepted gladly and told him to come as soon as possible. If he stayed alive until the next day, the girl would be his bride.

The dwarf went running home, took his friend, and they both went together to the palace.

At night, when the fisherman's boy entered the room with the Emperor's daughter, the dwarf went in with them and sat on the floor.

Overnight, the dwarf woke up, removed his friend from the bed, took out his own sword, and started his watch. It wasn't long before a great dragon came out of the girl. As soon as the dwarf saw it, *snap!* He cut off the head of the beast with the sword.

Afterwards, he woke his sworn brother and said, "Do you remember our deal, brother? Whatever we have, we'll share in half."

"Indeed," answered the boy.

And the dwarf went toward the girl, with the sword in his hand, threatening her that he would cut her in two, so he could have his half.

The girl gasped from fright and spit out an egg. The dwarf threatened her twice more, and two more eggs were out.

"Now," he said, "take your wife and be well. Before I killed the dragon, it made three more eggs, for three more dragons."

And then he told the boy that he was the fish his father had caught. Because the boy had set him free, he promised to do him well, so he gave the boy wealth and made him an Emperor's son-in-law.

"And now," he added, "take care of your bride and wealth and stay well."

As soon as he said that, he disappeared.

When the day came, so did the Emperor and saw them safe and unharmed. He was so happy; everybody was so happy! They celebrated in laughter and songs for seven days and seven nights.

*I was also there, and the sun shone over me.*
*I ate*
*I got bloated*
*And remained fat,*
*Like a pregnant cricket.*

# Dawn, Twilight, and Midnight

In a certain kingdom lived a king who had three beautiful daughters. The king guarded them more carefully than his own eyes. He built an underground palace in which he placed them, like birds in a cage, so that the boisterous winds wouldn't blow on them, and the bright sun wouldn't burn them with its rays.

Once, by some chance, the princesses read in a book that a wondrous white world[3] existed. When the king came to visit them, they immediately began to beg him, "Father, let us see the white world. Let us walk in the green gardens."

The king tried to dissuade them, but the more he refused, the more they insisted. Nothing could be done! He granted their request.

The princesses went into the garden to walk. They marveled at the bright sun, the trees, and the flowers. They were unspeakably delighted that the white world was available to them. They ran through the garden, amused themselves, and admired every blade of grass. All at once, a stormy whirlwind seized them and bore them high up and far away to an unknown location.

The nurses and governesses became terrified. The king sent his most trusty servants in every direction, promising a great reward to anyone who would find his daughters.

The king's messengers traveled far and wide but discovered nothing. What they went with, that they came back with. The king summoned a council and asked his knights if any of them would undertake a journey to find his daughters. He asked once, but all was silent; a second time, and no answer; a third time, and not half a word.

The king wept bitter tears and said, "I have no friends or defenders."

---

[3] "White world" refers to the realm of the living, while "dark world" refers to the land of the dead or the place where dragons live.

Then he ordered a proclamation to be made to the entire kingdom, hoping someone might be found among the common men to perform the task.

In a certain village lived a poor widow who had three sons, strong, mighty heroes. They were all born on the same night—the eldest at twilight, the second at midnight, and the third at dawn. On this account, they were named Twilight, Midnight, and Dawn. As soon as they heard of the king's proclamation, they received their mother's blessing and set out for the capital city.

The brothers came to the king, bowed before him, and said, "Hail, King! Be well for many years. We've come, not to feast, but to accomplish a good deed. Permit us to go and find your daughters."

"Honor to you, good youths. What are your names?"

"We are three brothers—Dawn, Twilight, and Midnight."

"What can I give you for your journey?"

"We need nothing for ourselves, O King, but don't desert our mother. Care for her in her poverty and old age."

The king sent for the old woman, lodged her in the palace, and gave orders she should eat and drink from the food off his own table and wear clothing from his own supply.

The three young men departed. They traveled one, two, and three months, until they came to a broad desert. Beyond it was a forest, and at the edge of the forest, a hut. When they arrived at the hut, they knocked but received no answer. They went in, but no one was there.

"Well, brothers," said Twilight, "let's rest here after our long journey."

They lay down to sleep. The next morning, the youngest brother, Dawn, said to Twilight, the eldest, "Midnight and I are going hunting, but you should stay here in case we don't catch anything, so you can make us something to eat."

Twilight agreed. Near the hut was a pen full of sheep. Not thinking long whether it was right or wrong, Twilight killed, dressed, and roasted the best sheep for their dinner. When everything was ready, he lay on a bench to rest.

All at once, a thumping and thundering occurred outside. The door opened and in came a little old man not quite four feet tall, with a beard twenty-six feet long trailing behind him.

He looked angrily at Twilight and screamed, "How dare you pretend to be the master of my house? How dare you kill my sheep?"

"Grow up, little man," answered Twilight. "I can't see you. I could blind you with a spoonful of soup and a bit of bread."

The little old man erupted with anger. "I'm small, but I'm strong."

He seized a club and beat Twilight until he was almost dead. The little old man threw Twilight under the bench, ate the roasted sheep, and retreated into the forest.

Twilight bound up his head with a cloth and lay on the bench, groaning.

When his brothers returned to the hut, they asked, "What happened to you?"

"Oh, brothers," he said, "I heated the stove, but then my head began to ache from the great fire. The heat was so great I couldn't roast any meat or make a stew."

The next day, Dawn went to hunt with Twilight, and they left Midnight at home to cook the dinner. He made a fire, picked out the fattest sheep, killed, dressed and roasted it, then lay on the bench. All at once, a thumping and thundering occurred outside. The door opened and in came a little old man not quite four feet tall, with a beard twenty-six feet long trailing behind him.

"How dare you pretend to be the master of my house and kill my sheep?" he screamed.

Flying at Midnight, the little old man beat and pounded Midnight until he was barely alive. Then the little old man ate the sheep and went into the forest. Midnight bound up his head and lay groaning on the bench.

When his brothers returned to the hut, they asked, "What happened to you?"

"When I kindled a fire in the stove, the heat stifled me. I couldn't make a roast or a stew, so we have nothing to eat."

The third day, the eldest brothers went to hunt, and Dawn stayed in the hut. He selected the best sheep, killed, dressed, and roasted it for dinner, then lay on the bench. All at once, a thumping and thundering occurred outside. Dawn looked out the window to see what was happening.

A little old man walked into the yard with a bundle of hay on his head and a pail of water in his hand. He put down the pail, scattered the hay over the yard, and counted his sheep. Soon he discovered one was missing. He flew into a rage, rushed into the hut, hurled himself at Dawn, and struck him heavily on the head.

Dawn sprang up, seized the little old man by the beard, and pulled and dragged him across the floor. As Dawn tugged, he kept saying, "Before measuring the depth of the ford, don't jump in."

The old man, not quite four feet tall, with a beard twenty-six feet long trailing behind him, began to beg, "Have mercy on me, mighty hero! Don't kill me. I'm sorry."

Dawn dragged the little old man into the yard and fastened his beard to an oak post with a great iron wedge. Then Dawn went back into the hut and waited for his brothers.

When they arrived, Dawn said, "I've caught 'heat' and fastened it to a post."

The brothers went into the yard and discovered that the little old man had run away, but half his beard was still attached to the post. Drops of blood lay scattered along the path the man had taken.

The brothers followed until they came to a deep opening in the ground. Dawn made a long rope, from the inner bark of trees and commanded his brothers to let him down to the underworld. They did so. When Dawn reached the bottom, he freed himself from the rope and went in the direction his eyes looked.

After traveling a long time, Dawn reached a copper palace. When he entered, a young princess greeted him and asked, "How have you come here? Was it of your own free will or against your will?"

"The king sent us to find you and your sisters," Dawn said.

Right away, she seated him at a table, gave him food and drink, and brought a flask of the Water of Strength. "Drink this water," she said. "Your strength will increase."

Dawn emptied the flask and felt his strength grow mightily. "Now," he thought, "I can overpower anything."

That moment, a terrible wind rose up, and the princess shivered with fright. "The dragon that stole me from my father is coming and will fly in here at any moment."

She took Dawn by the hand and hid him in another room.

A three-headed dragon came, hit the damp earth, and cried out, "There's a Russian odor here. Who's visiting you?"

"Who could find this place?" said the princess. "You've been flying through Russia. That's where you got the odor."

The dragon asked for meat and drink, which the princess brought. Into the wine, she poured a few drops of the Water of Sleep. The dragon ate and drank his fill, then fell asleep.

The princess called to Dawn. He came out of hiding immediately, drew his sword, and cut off the dragon's heads. Then he and the princess burned up the body and scattered the ashes over the open field.

Dawn left the princess and journeyed until he approached a silver palace. In that palace, lived the second princess. There Dawn killed a six-headed dragon, scattered his ashes, and went farther. Whether it was long or short, he made his way to a golden palace and found the eldest princess. He killed the twelve-headed dragon who lived there.

The princess rejoiced and got ready to go home with the hero. She went into the courtyard and waved a bright kerchief. The golden kingdom folded into an egg, which she put into her pocket. She then traveled with Dawn to get her sisters. They did as she had done, folding the silver and copper kingdoms into eggs and putting them into their pockets.

Dawn took the princesses to the opening to the upper world, and Twilight and Midnight drew up their brother and the women. When the brothers arrived back in their own country, the sisters unrolled the three eggs onto a wide, open space. Behold! The three kingdoms appeared—the copper, the silver, and the golden. The king was so delighted that his joy couldn't be told. Immediately, he married Twilight, Midnight, and Dawn to his three daughters, and he made Dawn heir of his kingdom.

# THE CASTLE IN CLOUDLAND

O nce upon a time, there lived a Tsar who had three sons and one daughter. The latter he brought up behind lock and key, and he guarded her like the very apple of his eyes. When the maiden grew up, she begged her father one evening to allow her to take a little stroll with her brothers. The Tsar permitted her to do so. But hardly had the four stepped out of the castle gate, when a dragon came flying along, seized the princess, and carried her away from the midst of her brothers, up into the clouds. As quickly as they could, the brothers hurried to their father and told him what had happened. They implored him to let them go search for their sister. The Tsar approved, gave a horse to each of them and everything else necessary for the long journey. Then the brothers started their quest.

After a long journey, they spotted a castle that was built neither on the earth nor in the sky, but appeared to hover among the clouds. When they came nearer, they wondered if it was possible that the young princess had been carried there. They discussed the matter as to how they could get up to her. After much careful reflection and discussion, they decided to kill one of their horses, cut its hide into strips, make a very long thong, fasten an arrow to the extreme end, and shoot it upward into the castle. After that, if the arrow held fast, they would climb up the thong.

The two younger brothers asked the eldest to kill his horse, but he refused. The second likewise didn't consent to the deed. The youngest, seeing it couldn't be helped, killed his horse, made a lengthy thong out of the hide, fixed an arrow to one end, and shot it straight up into the castle, where the arrow stuck firmly.

Next, they discussed who would have to climb up. Again, the two elder brothers refused, and only the youngest was ready to do it. Being agile, the youngest brother soon arrived in the castle above. He wandered from one room to another. At last, he entered an apartment, where, to his great joy, he found his sister. She was sitting on a couch. The dragon had put down his head into her lap and slept.

When she beheld her brother, she feared for his life and begged him urgently to escape before the dragon woke up. He ignored her pleas. Instead, he seized his club, whirled it around, and struck the dragon on the head.

The dragon, however, heavy with sleep, touched the spot with his claw and said to the trembling princess, "Something bit me here."

Once more, the prince gave the beast a second blow, but again the dragon only murmured, "Again, something has bitten me."

When the prince lifted up his arm to strike a third time, his sister pointed out to him the only spot where the dragon could be mortally wounded. The moment the club touched the spot, the dragon lay dead. The princess threw him down from her lap, leaped up, hastened to embrace and kiss her brother, and thanked him for her deliverance.

Then she took him by the hand to show him all the rooms of the castle one after another. First, she led him into a room, in which stood a black steed tied to a stall. The horse's harness and saddle were adorned with pure silver. Next, she led him into a second room. There, tied to its stall and ready to be mounted, stood a white horse that had a harness of pure gold. At last, she led him into a third room. There stood by the stall a beautiful Arab steed whose saddle, stirrups, and bridle were studded with precious stones.

Out of this room, she then led him into an apartment in which a maiden was sitting, bending over a golden frame, embroidering with golden threads. Next, she led him into another, where a maiden sat spinning golden threads. Finally, she led him into a room where a third maiden was threading pearls. In front of her a golden hen with its chickens was pecking at the pearls on a golden plate.

After they had been around in this fashion for a time and inspected everything, the princess returned to where the dragon lay dead, pulled him out of the room, and together with her brother, threw the carcass down to earth. Her two brothers below were almost mad with terror, so awful was the sight of the dragon.

The youngest brother first lowered his sister, then the three maidens one after another, each with her handiwork. While he was hard at work, he shouted to his brothers and made gestures indicating to whom each of the girls should belong. When it was the third maiden's turn—the maiden who had the golden hen and the chickens—he declared, "She's to be mine!"

The brothers, however, were envious that he had been such a hero and found and delivered their sister. They, therefore, cut the thong, so that the youngest brother was unable to come down himself. They took their sister, the maidens, and all the booty and hurried away.

On the way home, the princes met a shepherd watching his sheep. They convinced him to disguise himself and impersonate their youngest brother, and then they went home to their father. They strictly forbade their sister and the three maidens from saying anything of the true state of things.

After some time, the youngest brother, who remained in the castle, heard that his brothers and the shepherd were making preparations to marry the maidens he had delivered. On the day when the eldest brother's wedding was to take place, the youngest brother mounted the black steed, flew down, and landed in front of the church. When the wedding guests were leaving the church, and, as his brother was preparing to mount his horse, the youngest brother swiftly approached, raised his club and struck his brother so heavy a blow that he fell instantly to the ground, dazed. The youngest brother flew back to his castle on his black steed before anyone could apprehend him.

When he learned that the second brother was about to marry, the youngest brother came flying along seated on the white horse. After the wedding guests left the church, and his brother was about to mount his horse, the youngest brother approached and struck the bridegroom's shoulder, so that he at once fell to the ground, moaning and groaning. Once again, the youngest brother raced away back to the castle before he could be captured.

Eventually, news came that the shepherd was going to marry the maiden the youngest brother had chosen for his own. The young prince then mounted the Arab, landed in the churchyard as the wedding guests were leaving the church. He struck such a heavy blow on the bridegroom's head that the man fell down dead.

The wedding guests made a rush to catch the youngest brother, but he had no desire to escape this time. He revealed that he, and not the shepherd, was the Tsar's youngest son. He told them how the two wicked brothers, out of envy, had deserted him in the castle where he had found his sister and killed her captor. His sister and the three maidens immediately confirmed the prince's tale.

When the Tsar heard this, he was so infuriated with his two elder sons that he sent them into exile. Then the Tsar married the youngest son to his chosen bride. When the old Tsar died in a short time, the youngest prince became his successor, and the new Tsar and his beautiful bride lived happily ever after.

# THE SEVEN STARS

Once upon a time, there was a King who had a wonderfully beautiful daughter. But a Dragon came and stole her away, vanishing without a trace.

The King called his High Chamberlain and commanded him to go into the world and look for the Princess, and on no account to come back without her.

The High Chamberlain set out and searched throughout the whole world, but nowhere could he find the slightest trace of the King's daughter nor the least clue to her whereabouts. However, an old woman advised him to go to such and such a country and ask for the Dragon-mother, because she alone could give him information about the stolen Princess.

And so, the High Chamberlain followed her advice. After a troublesome journey, he at last arrived safely at the Dragon-mother's house and begged her to tell him what information she had about the location of the King's daughter.

The Dragon-mother answered, "My dear friend, stay here overnight. We'll share with you what we have; you won't go hungry in my house. As soon as my sons, the Dragons, return home from a distant journey, I'll ask them about the Princess. I have five sons, each one wiser and cleverer than the other. The first has the power of stealing anything that he takes a fancy to; he could steal the calf from the cow or the foal from the mare, and they'd never realize it. The second can follow the path of any lost object, even if it's been lost for years. The third shoots a straight arrow on anything he can see. The fourth can build an impregnable fortress in an instant and can hide anything he chooses within it, so that no one can possibly find it. And the fifth is as bold as a falcon and as swift as lightning when there's anything to be overtaken and caught."

While she was speaking, her sons, the Dragons, returned home. The mother asked them if they knew anything of the whereabouts of the King's lost daughter.

"To be sure," they answered. "She's with a more powerful Dragon than we. He stole her away from her father, the King, and now keeps her in one of his castles."

"I beg you," interrupted the High Chamberlain, "help me find her. I may on no account return to the King and live unless I bring his daughter with me. My master will be most grateful to you."

The Dragons said they were quite willing to help. The second brother located the scent, and the first brother stole the lovely maiden and brought her back with him. But the more powerful Dragon pursued them, took her away again, and flew up into the air to carry her to a safe place.

While the Dragon was flying away, the third brother fitted a bolt to his crossbow, drew it, and let the arrow fly. It hit the Dragon in the middle of his heart. With a fearful cry, the Dragon fell from the clouds and was dashed to bits on a rock. The King's daughter, whom the Dragon held tightly clasped, would have had the same fate, but the fifth brother flew swiftly and caught the maiden in the air, so that she was kept safe and sound.

But now the brothers encountered another danger. The dead Dragon's brother drew near, bringing several other monsters with him. It would soon have been all over with the brothers, but the fourth speedily built a strong fortress, in which all the brothers, the King's daughter, and the High Chamberlain safely concealed themselves.

For a long time, those hideous Dragons lay in wait around the fortress, but eventually they went away, having accomplished nothing. Then the five brothers, the gracious maiden, and the High Chamberlain came out and went home to the Dragon-mother.

The eldest son said, "Isn't it true, little mother, that the maiden belongs to me, since I rescued her from that furious Dragon?"

The second brother said, "But you would never have found her nor rescued her if I hadn't located the scent."

The third brother interrupted, "What good would it have been that you, eldest brother, rescued her, and you, second brother, found the scent, if I hadn't destroyed the monster at the right moment? Therefore, in all right and reason, the maiden belongs to me."

Here the fifth brother struck in. "By right, the maiden belongs to me. If I hadn't caught her in the nick of time, she wouldn't now be in the land of the living."

And the fourth brother said, "If you'll consider the whole matter impartially, you'll see that I have the most righteous claim to the maiden. All your trouble would have amounted to nothing if I hadn't made the castle at the right moment and hidden her, and you, too, within it."

And now the Chamberlain put in his word. "All your pretensions are idle. The maiden is mine. If I hadn't told you that she was stolen away, the first wouldn't have rescued her, nor the second located the scent, nor the third destroyed the monster, nor the fifth caught the maiden, nor would the fourth have concealed anyone in his castle."

Thus, all the six strove for possession of the maiden, until the Dragon-mother put in her word. "If this is so, then you are all in the right, but the maiden surely can't belong to you all. One thing you can do is you can all take her for your sister and love and protect her as long as you and she live."

And so, they did. In remembrance of the events, they and the maiden were set into the sky and can be seen there to this day. Men call them "the Seven Stars," the Pleiades. At least, that's how the story goes.

# THE WORLD–BEAUTIFUL
## SHARKAN ROJA

There was once in the world a great mythical kingdom, and in that kingdom a sorrowful king, who had a still more sorrowful wife. The king and queen were sorrowful because they didn't have children, although it was written in a magic book that they would have a son with golden teeth and magic power.

The queen once cried, "If I had a golden-toothed son with magic power, the world-beautiful Sharkan Roja would be his wife."

Seven years later, she gave birth to a golden-toothed son with magic power. No sooner was the boy born, when he spoke, saying, "Father, I want to learn; send me to school and give me a master."

When the boy was seventeen, he had finished every school in the world, and then he said to his mother, "Mother, do you remember what you promised before I was born?"

The queen had forgotten her promise.

"Try to think," repeated the magic youth, "what you promised before I was born."

Still the queen remembered nothing about it.

"I'll ask you once more. What did you promise before I was born?"

For the third time, the queen gave no answer. She thought as hard as she could, but she couldn't remember what she had promised.

"Well, mother," said the magic youth with a sigh, "I can't help it. I must make you remember."

He took an ax in his hand, struck the chief pillar of the palace, and split it open with a single blow. Then he fastened his mother's hair into the pillar's crack and left her there, saying, "You'll stay there until you tell me what you promised before I was born."

No one dared oppose the magic youth, although the king was there and with him were renowned heroes. They knew a thousand troubles would come to anyone who dared say anything, because the mighty youth had strength to crush them all with his little finger.

At last, the queen recalled what she had promised before her son was born, and she said, "Now, my dear son, I know what I promised. I cried out, 'If I had a golden-toothed son with magic power, the world-beautiful Sharkan Roja would be his wife.'"

"Very well, mother, you should have remembered that before to save yourself from disgrace. I couldn't help doing what I did. Now forgive me."

The magic youth drove the ax into the pillar, spread it open, took out his mother's hair, and freed her.

"But, my dear mother, why did you promise what you can't give? Why promise me the world-beautiful Sharkan Roja, who possesses immortal youth and unfading beauty? She's in the great dragon kingdom with her husband the King of the Dragons, who carried her off with violence from beautiful Wonderland. My own mother and my father who brought me up, I tell you this. While I can still see with my eyes, I'm going to travel until I find the Dragon Kingdom, even if I have to wear out my legs to the knees. I'll bring back the world-beautiful Sharkan Roja, or you'll never see me again, because I may end my life in that kingdom."

In the midst of a tearful farewell, the golden-toothed magic youth left his father, mother, and dear friends and set off to look for the world-beautiful Sharkan Roja. He traveled across forty-nine kingdoms until one day when darkness fell, he saw a light in the midst of a marsh. He approached the glow and beheld a wondrously beautiful woman sitting in a little golden coach. Six white squirrels were attached to it, but the coach was stuck in the mud. The squirrels could pull it neither one way nor the other.

The king's son quickly helped the six white squirrels, and with his aid, they got the coach out of the marsh. When the golden coach was on the dusty road, the wondrously fair lady turned to the magic youth and said, "Fair son of the king, expect good in return for good. What do you wish from me, the Queen of Wonderland?"

"I wish only this," answered the king's son. "Give me as wife the world-beautiful Sharkan Roja."

"Ah, prince, you're trying to move a big tree. Even though you haven't said who you are, still I know. Great is your power, great your knowledge, but you would be a small breakfast for the King of the Dragons. He kneads iron as I do dough, and crushes a rock as I do a bit of fresh cheese, and breaks down the largest tree of the forest with a stroke of his fist as easily as I break a hemp stalk. Therefore, if you try to move a great tree, you'll break your knife in it, and may easily lose your life."

"I'm not concerned about my life. If the Dragon King were seventy-seven times as strong, I'd still test my strength with him for Sharkan Roja."

"If you're so determined, know that Sharkan Roja is my daughter, and that dog's meat, the King of the Dragons, stole her from me. And know also that if you can bring her away, I'll take you as son, the beautiful Wonderland will be your home, and the world-beautiful Sharkan Roja will become your wife.

"Here are three golden hairs and a ragged strip of linen. Strike the three golden hairs with the ragged strip of linen, and you'll see what a splendid wind-bred, fire-eating, magic horse you'll have to carry you to the great Dragon Kingdom. The ragged bit of linen will become such a golden saddle that you'd never find elsewhere, even if you searched for one like it.

"When you're on your good horse, go to such and such a place, where a spring gushes forth from the foot of a great mountain. Bathe in that spring, and you'll find that although you were strong before, afterwards you'll be seven times stronger. No weapon will wound your body and your hair will become golden.

"When you've finished bathing, you'll find, in the grass near the spring, a sword growing out of the ground, its point upward. Pluck this sword, for it has the quality that, if your arm grows exhausted from excessive fighting, it strikes, thrusts, and kills by itself.

"If you do all this, perhaps you'll conquer the King of the Dragons. But if you feel your strength decreasing, here are three vials. Each of them contains a strengthening mixture. Drink from the smallest first, then from the middle, and finally from the largest one. From this drink, you'll regain your strength seven times stronger."

The Queen of Wonderland hit her squirrels with a golden whip and vanished like a dream, like a breath.

The prince struck, with the ragged piece of linen, the three hairs grown from one root. Like the swiftest lightning, there stood before him an iron-gray, six-legged, dragon-suckled, fire-eating, wind-bred magic horse, and the ragged linen turned into a golden saddle.

The king's son sat on the good horse and never stopped until he reached the foot of the great mountain, where he found a spring gushing forth. He bathed in the spring and his strength grew seven times stronger. When he had finished bathing, he looked for the sword growing out of the earth and found it. Then he sat on his good horse and went in search of the great Dragon Kingdom.

He traveled across forty-nine kingdoms until he came to a copper bridge. That bridge led to the Dragon Kingdom, and on it two dragons stood guard.

The king's son rested his good horse, then rushed toward the bridge. The dragons met him, but it wasn't long until the golden-haired, golden-toothed youth sent them to the other world.[4] They were no match for him and would have been small for his breakfast.

As the magic horse danced across the copper bridge, his golden shoes clattered. In this manner, the golden-toothed hero entered the great Dragon Kingdom. He hid himself by saying, "Cloud before me, cloud behind me that no one might see me."

And no one saw him even though he saw everything. Each dragon had his own palace of granite or marble, one more beautiful than the other. Each dragon also had a wife stolen from a king or count, or from Wonderland. Those palaces contained great mountains of plundered treasure—gold, silver, precious stones—and all kinds of costly weapons—swords with golden hilts, axes with boxwood handles. Three days wouldn't be enough for me to recount the plundered things piled up in the Dragon Kingdom.

A silken meadow stretched out in the middle of the kingdom. In the meadow was a garden where all the flowers of the earth bloomed without fading. Just then, dragons were cutting the silken grass with golden scythes, turning it with silver forks and gathering it with golden rakes. The silken grass was fodder for golden-haired horses. The golden-pillared diamond palace of the King of Dragons stood in the middle of the garden.

The king's son found the world-beautiful Sharkan Roja under a weeping willow. With eyes and mouth, he could not gaze on her shining beauty sufficiently. How could he? Her golden hair, plaited in two braids, touched her white feet and reached the earth; her body was like a bending reed; her gentle expression, like the look of a dove. When she smiled, roses bloomed on her tender face; when she wept, pearls fell from her eyes; and when she took a step, gold streamed from her heels.

The king's son put spurs to his good horse, rushed to Sharkan Roja, and said, "Why do you grieve, my heart's beautiful love? I've come to rescue you."

With that, they kissed each other, saying, "I'm yours. You're mine."

"My heart's heart," said the king's son, "is that dog of a dragon here?"

"My heart's beautiful love," answered Sharkan Roja, "he isn't here, but he'll come at noon."

"If he were here, I'd test my strength with him, but, my heart's heart, will you answer one question?"

"I will," said Sharkan Roja.

"Ah, my heart's golden love, my question is nothing else but this: can you tell me where the dragon's strength is?"

---

[4] The "other world" is a term that means the land of the dead.

"Oh, no! My heart's beautiful love. If I'd known where it was, you wouldn't have found me here."

"Can you tell me where his strengthening drink is, then?"

"In the cellar is a stone barrel, but I don't know what it contains. I can truthfully say, though, that the King of the Dragons goes to that barrel and drinks each noon."

"My heart's beautiful love, if I were to beg you, would you bring me some of that drink?"

Sharkan Roja took a golden cup, ran to the cellar, and brought back a full cup of wine from the stone barrel. The prince took a good long drink. Even though he had been strong before, he now became seven times stronger.

At noon, the King of the Dragons came home with a mighty clatter. When still far away, he shouted, "I smell a strange odor! I smell a strange odor!"

When he stopped in the courtyard, foam was dripping from his horse; it couldn't have dripped faster. The King of the Dragons didn't enter his palace, but called out in great anger, "I've heard about the fame of the golden-toothed magic prince. I'd fight with him if he were here."

"I'm here!" cried the prince.

"If you're here, you find me in good humor. Come to my lead driveway and we'll test each other's strength."

They went to the lead driveway. The King of the Dragons took a piece of rock and cut it in half with a wooden knife. One half he kept himself, and the other half he gave to the prince, saying, "If you can crush this stone as I do, then I'll believe you're strong."

The dragon squeezed the stone until it was like flour.

"That's nothing!" cried the golden-toothed hero. "I'll squeeze the rock so that not only will it become flour, but water will drip from it."

With that, he squeezed the rock until it was not merely dust, but water dripped from it.

"Now I see," said the dragon, "that you're strong and worthy to fight me. I'll go to the cellar for my sword, then we'll meet."

"You won't carry your dog shirt out of here! If you have no sword, I'll throw mine away and we'll fight unarmed."

What was the dragon to do? He realized he'd come across a worthy man. He seized the king's son by the waist and struck him into the lead driveway so that the king's son sank to his knees, but the prince wasn't slow. He sprang out of the hole, caught the dragon by the waist, and thrust him into the lead driveway up to the dragon's knees.

The dragon wasn't slow. He sprang out of the hole, caught the golden-toothed hero by the waist, and thrust him in up to his chin. But the golden-toothed hero wasn't slow. He sprang out of the hole, caught the dragon by the waist, and thrust him in up to the tip of his nose.

When the dragon couldn't get out, the hero said, "Well, King of the Dragons, do you believe now that I'm strong? I can take your life, but I'll spare you on one condition."

"What is it?"

"That you'll give me the world-beautiful Sharkan Roja."

"She's yours," said the dragon.

The golden-toothed hero wanted no more. In a moment, he sprang onto his good horse, took Sharkan Roja in his arms, and rode away. But he had barely reached the gate when the King of Dragons, who was out of the hole and had taken a long drink from the barrel, called, "Come back, golden-toothed hero. The world-beautiful Sharkan Roja isn't yours yet. I was kidding you. Now we'll have a real test of strength."

The prince's chin fell, for then did he know with whom he had to deal. He turned back, and they closed ranks with one another. First, the prince took a long drink from the three vials the Queen of Wonderland had given him. Not much time passed before the King of the Dragons bit the dust.

The world-beautiful Sharkan Roja struck the diamond palace three times with a golden rod, and all the treasures, the flowery garden, and the silken meadow turned into a diamond apple. She hid the apple close to her chest and sat on the magic horse by the side of her true love.

The golden-toothed magic youth took Sharkan Roja to his father's kingdom. Great was the joy throughout the kingdom when the hero returned with his bride. It was still greater when the world-beautiful Sharkan Roja removed the diamond apple, put it down in the most beautiful part of the kingdom, struck it three times with the golden rod, and behold, in a flash, the silken meadow stretched out before them. In the middle of the meadow was the garden where all the flowers of the round world bloomed without fading, and in the middle of the garden was the gold-pillared diamond palace.

They held a wedding. The golden-toothed magic hero and the world-beautiful Sharkan Roja live in that palace yet, if they are not dead.

# IVAN THE PEASANT'S SON

**And the Little Man Himself One-finger Tall, His Mustache Seven Verts[5] in Length**

In a certain kingdom in a certain land there lived a Tsar. In the Tsar's courtyard was a pillar, and on the pillar three rings: one gold, one silver, and the third copper. One night, the Tsar dreamed a horse was tied to the gold ring. Every hair on the creature was silver, and the clear moon was on his forehead. In the morning, the Tsar rose and ordered it to be proclaimed that whoever could interpret the dream and get the horse for him, to that man he would give his daughter and one half the kingdom.

At the summons of the Tsar, a multitude of princes, knights, and all kinds of lords assembled. No man could explain the dream; no man would undertake to get the horse. At last, they explained to the Tsar that such and such a poor man had a son Ivan, who could interpret the dream and get the horse.

The Tsar commanded them to summon Ivan. When Ivan arrived, the Tsar asked, "Can you explain my dream and get the horse?"

"Tell me first," answered Ivan, "what the dream was, and what horse you need."

The Tsar said, "Last night I dreamed a horse was tied to the gold ring in my courtyard; every hair on him was silver, and the clear moon was on his forehead."

"That's not a dream, but reality. Last night a twelve-headed dragon came to you on that horse and wanted to steal your daughter."

"Is it possible to get that horse?"

"It is," answered Ivan, "but only after my fifteenth birthday."

Ivan was at the time only twelve years old. The Tsar brought Ivan to his court and gave him food and drink until he turned fifteen.

After his fifteenth birthday, Ivan said to the Tsar, "Now give me a horse on which I can ride to the place where the dragon lives."

---

[5] A verts is a little over a half a mile. The measurements have been converted in the story.

The Tsar led him to his stables and showed him all his horses. Ivan couldn't find a single one suitable for his strength and weight. When he placed his hero's hand on any horse, that horse fell to the ground.

Ivan said to the Tsar, "Let me go to the open country to seek a horse that's strong enough to carry me."

The Tsar let him go. Ivan the peasant's son looked for three years. Nowhere could he find a horse. He was returning to the Tsar in tears, when an old man happened to meet him, and asked, "Why are you crying, young man?"

Ivan answered the old man rudely and chased him away.

The old man said, "Be careful, young fellow. Don't speak ill of me."

Ivan went away a little from the old man and thought, "Why have I offended the old man? Old people know much."

He returned, caught up with the old man, fell on his face before him, and said, "Grandfather, forgive me! I offended you because of my unhappiness. I'm crying because I've traveled for three years through the open country among many herds. I can't find a horse to suit me anywhere."

The old man said, "Go to such a village. In a poor peasant's stable, you'll find a mare that has a mangy colt. Get the colt and feed him. He'll be strong enough for you."

Ivan bowed to the old man and went to the village. He went straight to the peasant's stable. When he saw the mare with the mangy colt, he put his hands on the colt. The colt didn't quiver in the least. Ivan bought him from the peasant and fed the colt for some time. Then Ivan returned to the Tsar, said he had a horse, and began preparations to visit the dragon.

The Tsar asked, "How many men do you need, Ivan?"

"I need no men," replied Ivan. "I can get there with only my horse. You could give me perhaps half a dozen men to relay messages."

The Tsar gave him six men, who got ready and set out with Ivan. Whether they travelled long or short, it's unknown to any man. Only this is known: they came to a fiery river. Over the river was a bridge, and near the river, an enormous forest. In that forest they pitched a tent, got many things to drink, and began to eat and enjoy themselves.

Ivan the peasant's son said to his companions, "Let's take turns keeping watch every night. I want to see if any man crosses the river."

Every time any of Ivan's companions had guard duty, each one got drunk in the evening and saw nothing. At last, it was Ivan's turn to watch. Exactly at midnight, he saw a three-headed dragon cross the river.

The dragon called, "I have no enemy, no slanderer, except for Ivan the peasant's son, but the raven hasn't brought his bones to me in a bladder yet."

Ivan the peasant's son sprang from under the bridge. "You liar, I'm here!"

"If you're here, then let's fight."

The dragon advanced on horseback against Ivan, but Ivan met him on foot. Ivan struck the dragon with a mighty blow from his sword and cut off all three heads. He took the horse for himself and tied it to the tent.

The next night Ivan the peasant's son killed a six-headed dragon, and the third night a nine-headed one. He threw each of them into the fiery river.

When he went on guard the fourth night, a twelve-headed dragon came and began to speak angrily, "Where are you, Ivan the peasant's son? Come out this minute to me! Why did you kill my sons?"

Ivan the peasant's son slipped out and said, "Let me go first into my tent, and then I'll fight with you."

"Well, go on."

Ivan ran to his companions. "Here, men, is a bowl. Keep watching it while I fight. When it fills with blood, come help me."

He returned and stood opposite the dragon. They rushed forward and struck each other. Ivan's first blow cut off four of the dragon's heads, but he himself sank up to his knees into the ground. When he struck the dragon a second time, Ivan cut off three more heads and sank up to his waist. The third time they met, he cut off three more heads and sank up to his breast. At last, he cut off one head and sank up to his neck in the ground.

Only then did his companions remember him. They looked into the bowl and saw blood flowing over the edge. They hurried out, cut off the dragon's last head and pulled Ivan out of the earth. Ivan took the dragon's horse and led it to the tent.

Night passed, morning came. The youths began to eat, drink, and enjoy themselves. Ivan the peasant's son rose up from the merry-making and said to his companions, "Wait here."

He turned into a cat and crept along the bridge over the fiery river. He traveled until he came to the house where the dragons used to live, and began to make friends with the cats there. In the house, there remained alive only the old mother of the dragons and her three daughters-in-law.

The females were sitting in the room talking to one another. "How can we destroy that scoundrel, that Ivan the peasant's son?"

The youngest daughter-in-law said, "I'll make them hungry while they travel. Then I'll turn myself into an apple tree, so that when he eats an apple, it'll tear him to pieces in a moment."

The second daughter-in-law said, "I'll make them thirsty while they travel. Then I'll turn myself into a well and let him try to drink."

71

The eldest said, "I'll make them tired and then turn myself into a bed. When Ivan tries to lie down, he'll die in a minute."

Finally, the old woman said, "I'll open my mouth from earth to sky and swallow them all."

Ivan heard what they said, left the room, turned into a man, and returned to his companions. "Now, boys, let's get ready to travel."

They got ready and went on their way. Along the road, they began to have a ravishing hunger, but had nothing left to eat. They saw an apple tree. Ivan's companions wanted to pluck the fruit, but Ivan wouldn't let them.

"That's not an apple tree," he said. He slashed at the tree, and blood poured out.

As they continued their journey, they all became terribly thirsty, but their water was low. Ivan saw a well, but he wouldn't let anyone drink from it. He slashed at it until blood poured out.

After walking farther, everyone started yawning. A bed lay ahead on the side of the road, and the men begged Ivan to stop so they could sleep. He forbade them, and he cut the bed to pieces until blood soaked the ground.

Soon after that, they saw ahead of them jaws stretching from the earth to the sky. What could they do? The men contemplated running their horses fast and jumping over the obstacle. Not one of them was able to jump over the jaws except Ivan, because he was carried out of trouble by his wonderful steed, every hair of which was silver, and the bright moon on his forehead.

Ivan came to a river and saw a hut. Outside stood a little man, four and a half inches tall, with a mustache four and a half miles long.

The little man said, "Give me your horse. If you won't give it voluntarily, I'll take him by force."

Ivan answered, "Leave me, cursed reptile, or I'll crush you under the horse."

The little man, four and a half inches tall, with a mustache four and a half miles long, knocked Ivan to the ground, sat on the horse, and rode away. Ivan went into the hut and grieved greatly for his stolen horse. In the hut, a footless, handless man was lying on a mat on the stove.[6]

The man said to Ivan, "Listen, good hero, I don't know your name. Why did you try to fight with him? I was more of a hero than you, and still he gnawed my hands and feet off."

"Why?"

---

[6] It was customary for peasants to sleep on the stove on mats after the heat was turned off at night.

"Because I ate bread at his table."

Ivan asked how he could win his horse back.

The footless, handless man said, "Go to such a river and take charge of the ferry. Travel on the ferry for three years, but don't take money from anyone. After that, you'll be able to win the horse back."

Ivan bowed to the man, went to the river, got on the ferry, and ferried three whole years for no pay. Once he happened to ferry three old men across the river. They offered him money, but he refused to take it.

"Tell me, good hero, why won't you take any money?"

He said, "Because of a promise."

"What promise?"

"A malicious man took my horse, and a good man told me to take charge of the ferry for three years, without receiving money from any man."

The old men said, "If you want, Ivan, we're ready to help you get back your horse."

"Yes, please. Help me, my friends."

The old men were not ordinary people: they were the Freezer, the Devourer, and the Wizard.

The Wizard went to the shore, made a picture of a boat in the sand, and said, "Well, brothers, you see this boat?"

"We see it."

"Sit in it."

All four sat in the boat.

The Wizard said, "Now, light little boat, do me a favor as you did before."

Straighatway, the boat rose into the air, and in a flash, just like an arrow sent from a bow, it brought them to a great stony mountain. At that mountain stood a house, and in the house lived the little man, four and a half inches tall, with a mustache four and a half miles long. The old men sent Ivan to ask for the horse.

The little man said, "Steal the Tsar's daughter and bring her to me, then I'll give you the horse."

Ivan told his companions what had to be done. They left Ivan at once and went to the Tsar.

The Tsar knew what they had come for and commanded his servants to heat the bath[7] red hot. "Let them suffocate in there."

Then he asked his guests to the bath. They thanked him and went. The Wizard commanded the Freezer to go first. The Freezer went into the bath

---

[7] Bath here refers to a *banya*, which is like a sauna.

and made it cooler. Then the three men washed and steamed themselves, then returned to the Tsar.

The Tsar ordered a great dinner to be given, and a multitude of all kinds of food was set on the table. He commanded the men to eat it all or lose their lives. The Devourer began and ate everything.

In the night, the men came together, stole the Tsar's daughter, and brought her to the little man, four and a half inches tall, with a mustache four and a half miles long. They gave him the Tsar's daughter and got the horse in return.

Ivan bowed down to the old men, sat on the horse, and returned to the Tsar. He traveled and traveled, stopped in an open field to rest, put up his tent, and lay down. When he woke up, he threw out his hand, because the Tsar's daughter was beside him.

Delighted, he asked, "How did you get here?"

"I turned into a pin and stuck myself into your collar."

She turned into a pin again after speaking. Ivan stuck her into his collar and traveled on to the Tsar. The Tsar saw the wondrous horse, received the good hero with honor, but lamented how his daughter had been stolen.

Ivan said, "Don't grieve. I've brought her back."

He went into the next chamber, where the Tsarevna turned into a fair maiden. Ivan took her by the hand and brought her to the Tsar.

The Tsar rejoiced greatly. He took the horse for himself and gave his daughter to Ivan. Ivan is living yet with his young wife.

# The Dragon and the Gypsy

In the old days, there was a village. A dragon made it a habit to fly to that village and devour the people who lived there. He ate everyone; only one man was left. At that time, a gypsy arrived there; it was late in the evening. Everywhere he looked, he saw empty huts! Eventually, he entered the last hut and saw a man who was sitting there crying.

"Hello, kind man!"

"Why are you here, gypsy? Are you tired of life?"

"Why?"

"Because the dragon has made a habit of flying to our village and devouring the people. He's eaten everyone, but he's left me alone until the morning. Tomorrow, he'll fly here to devour me, and it won't be good for you, either. He'll eat both of us at once!"

"Or maybe he'll choke!" replied the gypsy. "Let me spend the night here with you. Tomorrow we'll see what kind of dragon is flying here."

They spent the night.

In the morning, a severe storm suddenly arose. The hut shook as a dragon flew in.

"Aha!" he said. "I've made a profit! I left one man and found two. I'll have something for breakfast as well!"

"Will you really eat us?" asked the gypsy.

"Yes, I'll eat you!"

"You lie, you damn thing! You'll choke!"

"Why? Do you think you're stronger than I am?"

"I sure am!" replied the gypsy. "Don't you know that I have more strength than you do?"

"Well, let's see who's stronger."

"Come on!"

The dragon took out a rock from the grindstone. "Look, gypsy! I'll crush this rock with one hand."

"Okay, I'm watching!"

The dragon took the rock in his hands and squeezed it so tight that it turned into fine sand: sparks fell down!

"What a miracle!" said the gypsy with sarcasm. "Can you squeeze the rock so that water flows out of it? See how I can squeeze it!"

There was a bundle of cottage cheese on the table. The gypsy grabbed it and started squeezing so the whey flowed to the ground.

"Did you see that? Who has more strength?"

"Okay, your hands are stronger than mine," the dragon replied, "but let's see who can whistle harder?"

"Okay, go ahead and whistle!"

The dragon whistled so hard that leaves fell off of all the trees.

"All right, brother, you whistled quite well, but you're not better than I am," said the gypsy. "Why don't you tie your blinkers up beforehand? Otherwise, when I whistle, they'll fall out of your forehead!"

The dragon believed him and tied his eyes with a handkerchief. "Well, go ahead and whistle!"

The gypsy took a bat and hit the dragon on the head as hard as he could.

The dragon shouted at the top of his lungs, "That's enough! Stop it, gypsy! Don't whistle anymore. After only one whistle, my eyes almost fell out."

"As you wish, but I'm very likely ready to whistle once or twice more."

"No, don't. I don't want to argue anymore. Instead, let's fraternize with each other: you'll be the older brother, and I'll be the younger."

"Okay, maybe we can do that!"

"Well, brother," said the dragon, "go. There's a herd of oxen grazing on the prairie; choose the fattest one, grab it by the tail, and bring it for lunch."

The gypsy had no choice. He went to the prairie. He saw a large herd of oxen grazing. He started catching them and tying them together by their tails.

The dragon waited and waited, and when he couldn't wait anymore, he ran to the prairie himself. "What's taking you so long?"

"Wait. I'll tie fifty oxen together and will drag them all home, so it'll last us the whole month!"

"Aren't you a smarty! That will make us stay here forever! One ox will be enough."

Then the dragon grabbed the fattest ox by the tail, pulled the skin off it, loaded the meat onto its shoulders, and dragged it home.

"Come on, brother. I tied so many oxen together. It's a shame to leave them like that."

"Just leave them."

They came back to the hut, filled two cauldrons with beef, but there was no water.

"Here, take the ox's skin," the dragon said to the gypsy. "Go and fill it with water and bring it back; let's cook dinner."

The gypsy took the skin and dragged it to the well. He could barely drag it when it was empty, let alone with water. He started digging around the well.

The dragon waited and waited, and when he couldn't wait anymore, he ran to the well himself. "What are you doing, brother?"

"I want to dig the well all out and bring the whole thing into the hut so we don't have to walk for water."

"What are you, smarty pants? You're trying to do a lot! It takes a lot of time to dig."

The dragon sank the skin into the well, filled it with water, pulled it out, and carried it home.

"And you, brother," he said to the gypsy, "go to the woods for now, choose a dry oak, and drag it into the hut; it's time to start a fire!"

The gypsy went into the woods, started to tear bark and make ropes. He twisted a long, long rope and started to ensnare the oaks.

The dragon waited and waited, and when he couldn't wait anymore, he ran to the woods himself. "Why are you so slow?"

"Well, I want to tie together with a rope twenty oak trees at a time and drag them along with the roots so we'll have enough firewood for a long time!"

"Aren't you a smarty! You're doing everything your way," said the dragon. He pulled out the thickest oak tree and dragged it to the hut.

The gypsy pretended to be very angry, pouted, and sat in silence.

The dragon cooked the beef and started calling the gypsy for dinner, but the gypsy answered him resentfully, with his heart on his sleeve, "I don't want anything!"

The dragon ate the entire ox, drank all the water from the ox skin, and asked the gypsy, "Tell me, brother, why are you mad?"

"Because no matter what I do, everything is wrong. Nothing is your way!"

"Well, don't be angry. Let's make up!"

"If you want to make peace with me, let's go to my place."

"No problem. I'm ready, brother!"

Immediately, the dragon took out a cart, harnessed three of his best horses, and they went together to the gypsy's camp.

When they got closer, the young gypsies saw their father, and started running toward him. Naked, they shouted at the top of their lungs, "Father has arrived and brought the dragon!"

The dragon got scared and asked the gypsy, "Who are they?"

"Oh, those are my children! Looks like they're really hungry. Watch out, they might eat you!"

The dragon jumped off the cart and ran away. The gypsy sold the three horses along with the cart and lived happily ever after.

# Peerless Beauty, the Cake-Baker

In a far-off land lived a Tsar and a Tsaritza who had one son, whom they named Ivan. They were delighted when he was born and placed him in a beautiful oaken cradle among pillows of the softest down, covering him with a little eider-down quilt of silk from Samarcand. The pillow on which rested his little head was ornamented with drawn-thread work and all was cosy and comfortable. Even so, try as they would, the nurse-maidens—and they were pretty ladies of the highest degree—could not rock Ivan Tsarevich to sleep. Softly they sang and sweetly they crooned, but the young prince roared lustily, tossed off the coverlet, kicked out the pillow, and beat the sides of the cradle with his little fists.

At last, the nurse-maidens lost all patience, and they cried out to the Tsar, "Little Father, Little Father, come and rock your own son."

The Tsar sat by the side of the cradle, placed his great toe upon the rocker, and said, "Sleep, little son, sleep, sleep, sleep. Soon you'll be a man, and then I'll get you Peerless Beauty as a bride. She's the daughter of three mothers, the granddaughter of three grandmothers, and the sister of nine brothers."

He made this promise once only, and it had such a soothing effect upon the restless Tsarevich that he went to sleep and continued sleeping for three days and three nights, during which time the nurse-maidens sat and praised his beauty among themselves. But they ceased talking as soon as he woke up again, for now he cried more loudly than ever, tossed off the coverlet, kicked out the pillow, and beat the sides of the cradle with his little fists.

Once again, the nurse-maidens tried to console him and to rock him to sleep, because they loved and admired him best in his slumbers. He refused to sleep, and they were forced to call out, "Little Father, Little Father, come and rock your own son."

The Tsar came once more to his son's cradle and made the wonderful promise, whereupon the child fell asleep again and slept for three days and three nights.

When he woke up, he was as naughty as before. For a third time, the nurse-maidens had to call in the help of the Little Father.

When the Tsarevich awoke the third time, he stood upon his cradle and said, "Bless me, Little Father, for I'm going to my wedding."

"My dear son," said the Tsar in great wonderment, "you're only nine days old. How can you marry?"

"That's how it is," said the Tsarevich, "and if you won't give me your blessing, I fear I must marry without it."

"Well, well," said the Tsar, "may all good go with you."

Then he was not in the least surprised to see his son step down from the cradle a full-grown youth of goodly shape. The young man called for clothes suitable to his age—they were all ready to hand over to him—and then went to the stables.

On the way across the courtyard, he met an old man, who looked at him and said, "Young man, where are you going?"

"Mind your own business," said the young prince. But when he had gone forward a little, he stopped and said to himself, "That was a mistake. Old people know many useful things." He turned around and went back to the old man.

"Stop, stop, grandfather," he said, "what did you ask me?"

"I asked you," said the ancient man, "where you were going. Now I'll add to my question. Are you going there of your own free will or against your will?"

"I'm going of my own free will," said the Tsarevich, "and twice as much against my will. I was in my cradle when my father came to me and promised to get me Peerless Beauty as a bride. She's the daughter of three mothers, the granddaughter of three grandmothers, and the sister of nine brothers. I suppose I must go to seek her."

"You're a courteous youth," said the old man, "and deserve to take advantage of the knowledge of the aged. You can't go on foot to seek out Peerless Beauty, because she lives at the edge of the white world at the place where the sun peeps up. It's called the Golden Kingdom of the East."

"What can I do?" asked the Tsarevich, thrusting his hands into his belt and standing with feet wide apart. "I have no brave horse or silk whip for such a ride."

"Why, your father has thirty of the best horses," said the old man, "and the trouble with you will be to make a wise choice. Go to the stables and tell the grooms to take the thirty to bathe in the deep blue sea. When they come to the shore, you'll see one of them push forward into the water up to its neck and drink. When this happens, watch carefully to see if the waves rise high and break into foam on the beach. If so, select that horse; it will take you safely to the edge of the white world and to the place where the sun peeps up, which is called the Golden Kingdom of the East."

"Thanks and thanks again, good grandfather," said the Tsarevich, who then went on to the stables and selected his heroic steed in the manner the old man had described. On the following morning, the Tsarevich was preparing his horse for the journey when it turned its head and spoke to him.

"Ivan Tsarevich," it said, "fall down on the lap of moist Mother Earth, and I'll push you three times."

The youth was so astonished to hear the horse speak that he found it easy enough to fall down. Then the horse pushed him once and pushed him a second time. After that, the horse looked at the youth for a little time and said, "That'll be enough. If I push you a third time, moist Mother Earth won't be able to hold you."

The Tsarevich rose to his feet, saddled his horse, and set out. His father and those around him saw him as he mounted, but they didn't see him as he rode. He appeared only like a smoke wreath on the open boundless plain, before he was gone. Far, far away he rode until the day grew short and the long night descended. As the darkness fell, the rider came to a house as large as a town, with rooms each as big as a village. At the great door, he dismounted and tied the bridle to a copper ring in the door-post. Then he went into the first room.

He said to an old woman he found there, "Blessings on this house. I'd be happy if you'd permit me to spend the night here."

"Where are you journeying?" asked the old woman.

"That's not the first question you should ask," said the Tsarevich. "Give me food to eat and wine to drink, then put me next into a warm sleeping chamber. In the morning, ask me whether I've slept in peace, and then ask where I may be journeying."

And the old woman did as he requested.

The next morning, when she asked him the second question, he replied, "I was in my cradle when my father promised to get me Peerless Beauty as a bride. She's the daughter of three mothers, the granddaughter of three grandmothers, and the sister of nine brothers."

"Good youth," said the old woman, "I'm nearly seventy years old, but I've never heard of Peerless Beauty. Farther on the way lives my elder sister. Perhaps she knows."

Then Ivan Tsarevich left the great house, and, after taking courteous leave of the old woman, rode far away across the open steppe. All day he rode, and as night was descending, he came to a second house as large as a town, with each room as large as a village. He dismounted, tied the bridle to a silver ring in the door-post, and asked an old woman he met in the first room if he might have a night's lodging. And here it happened as it had happened before, only the old woman was eighty years of age.

"Farther on the road," she said, "lives my elder sister, and she has givers of answers. The first givers of answers are the fishes and other dwellers in the heaving restless sea. The second givers of answers are the wild beasts of the dark forests. The third givers of answers are the birds of the open air. Whatever is in the whole white world is obedient to the will of my elder sister."

Once again, Ivan Tsarevich set out and came to a house where he tied his horse to a golden ring. He was received by an old, old woman, who screamed at him in a voice like a flock of peacocks, "Oh, you man of boldness, why have you tied your horse to a golden ring? Is an iron ring too good for you?"

"Patience, good grandmother," said the Tsarevich gently. "It's easy to loosen the bridle and tie the horse to another ring."

"Ah, my good youth," said the old woman gently, and as one would speak to a child, "did I frighten you? Sit down on the bench and have some food and drink."

Ivan did so, and then without being asked, he told the old woman where he was going and what was his quest.

"Go to your rest," she said shortly. "In the morning, I'll call my givers of answers."

The next morning, the old woman and the young man sat on the porch. The former gave a heroic whistle, at which the blue sea heaved in a great heap, and the fishes, large and small, sea-serpents and sea-dragons, rose up to the surface and made for the shore.

"Come no farther," said the old woman, raising her right hand. "Tell me where this good youth can find Peerless Beauty."

Then the answer came from a million mouths, "We haven't seen or heard of her."

The old woman blew her whistle and the forests echoed to the sound of a million voices of wild beasts, but the answer to her question was, "We haven't seen or heard of her."

"Come here," said the grandmother, "all you birds of the air."

In a moment, the light of the sun was hidden, and the sound of flapping wings was like a tempest. But the answer of the birds to the question was the same, "We haven't seen or heard of her."

"My givers of answers fail me," said the ancient woman as she took Ivan by the lily-white hand and led him into the house.

Then there flew through the open window the Mogol Bird, which fell to the ground at her feet.

"Ah, Mogol Bird," said the old woman, "where have you come from?"

"I come from the home of Peerless Beauty," was the tired reply, "and I've been dressing her for Mass in the Cathedral."

The old woman clapped her hands in delight. "That's the news I seek. Now, Mogol Bird, do me a favor. Carry this young man, Ivan Tsarevich, to the home of Peerless Beauty."

"That I will," was the reply, "but we'll need a great deal of food."

"How much?" asked the old woman.

"Three hundred pounds of beef," the Mogol Bird answered, "and a keg full of water."

Ivan filled a large keg with water and placed it on the back of the Mogol Bird with the heaped-up piles of beef around it. Then he ran to the forge and told the smith to make him a long iron lance. With this weapon in his hand, he sat on the edge of the keg with the beef all surrounding him. Up rose the Mogol Bird. Once it was on its way, it flew so steadily that the top of the water in the keg remained always level. Now and again, the bird would slowly turn its head and look at Ivan, who at once gave it a large piece of beef skewered on the point of his long iron lance.

Onward, and ever onward, flew the Mogol Bird, feeding on the beef and drinking the water from Ivan's cap, which he extended at the point of his lance, until all the meat and water were finished, at which point, the Tsarevich threw the keg overboard.

"Oh, Mogol Bird," he said, "hurry and finish your journey. There's no more beef and no more water."

"I can't go down to earth in this spot," said the bird. "Beneath us, there's nothing but a bog like glue. I must have more meat to continue. If you can't get beef, veal will do."

Ivan cut off the calves of his own legs. When the bird had refreshed itself, it flew on until it came to a green meadow with tall silken grass and blue flowers. Here it flew down to earth, and Ivan alighted, but, of course, walked quite lame.

"What makes you limp, Ivan Tsarevich?" asked the Mogol Bird.

When the young man told what he had done, the bird blew upon the back of his legs and restored him to his former condition.

On went the young man, eager to finish his quest. He came to a great town, where he entered a narrow street and found an old woman in a poor, mean house. She seemed to be expecting him.

"Go to bed and sleep soundly after your flight, Ivan," she said. "When the bell rings, I'll call you."

The young man lay down and slept soundly, so soundly that when the bell rang for early morning prayers, not all the calling, nor all the shaking, nor all the shouting, nor all the beating could rouse him. Then the bell rang again for Mass. The old grandmother tried once more, calling, shaking, shouting, beating, but all with no result, until she took a tiny feather and tickled the sleeper's nose. Then he awoke with a start, washed himself clean, dressed himself carefully, and went to Mass in the cathedral.

He bowed first to the high altar, then to North, South, East, and West, and especially to Peerless Beauty, who knelt alone in the church. Ivan Tsarevich knelt beside her and stood beside her while she prayed. When the service was over, the young man looked at Peerless Beauty, and looked again, and yet again without speaking. While he looked, six brave heroes came up from the seashore and stood at the great door of the cathedral. Peerless Beauty went to meet them with Ivan Tsarevich close behind her.

"What country clown is this?" cried the brave heroes.

Ivan stepped in front of Peerless Beauty and swung his right arm in a circle three times. When he stopped, the heroes were lying at the feet of the Princess in a heap of confusion.

Then Ivan Tsarevich returned to the old grandmother, who put him to bed. On the second day, it all happened as on the first occasion. Peerless Beauty looked at Ivan as he knelt in silence by her side, and as she looked, she blushed.

On the third day, it all happened as on the first in every particular except that when Ivan entered the church, Peerless Beauty gave him a silent greeting and then came and stood at his left side.

When the young man had laid low six more scornful heroes, Peerless Beauty took him by the hand, and together, without a word, they approached the priest and took the golden crowns of marriage. After that, they went home and feasted, and then prepared to set out for Ivan Tsarevich's home.

Over the open boundless plain they rode, speaking little, but looking much and smiling frequently, until Peerless Beauty grew weary and lay down to rest, while Ivan Tsarevich guarded.

When she awoke refreshed, the bridegroom said, "Now guard me while I sleep, Peerless Beauty. I'm quite weary."

"Will your sleep be short or long?" asked the bride.

"I'll sleep," said Ivan, "for no longer and no shorter than nine days and nine nights. If you try to rouse me, I won't wake up. When the end of the time comes, I'll wake without any help."

"I'll be weary of waiting and watching, Ivan Tsarevich," said Peerless Beauty with a sigh.

"Weary or not, it can't be changed," said Ivan Tsarevich. Then he lay down and slept for nine days and nine nights.

While he slept, a rushing whirlwind swept across the open steppe. In the center of the whirlwind, where there was the point of peace, rested Koschei Who Never Dies. The dragon bore away Peerless Beauty to his kingdom beyond the sea. And so, when Ivan Tsarevich awoke without any help, he found himself alone.

Sadly, he gazed across the empty boundless plain. When he arose, he returned to the town, sought out the old woman in the poor, mean house. Again, she seemed to be expecting him. He told her his entire tale of sadness.

"I had everything," he said, "and now I have nothing."

"Go to bed and sleep soundly after your sorrow, Ivan," she said.

He went to bed, but could sleep neither soundly nor restlessly. At midnight, a rushing whirlwind swept across the open steppe, and in the center of the whirlwind, where there was the point of peace, rested Koschei Who Never Dies. The whirlwind bore away Ivan Tsarevich to Koschei's kingdom beyond the sea.

At the gate of the palace, Ivan knocked—*tock, tock*—and Peerless Beauty opened the wicket-gate in the large gate. She peeped out with eyes like violets wet with the rain, and cheeks like roses in the morning sun, and a brow like a seed pearl of priceless luster. She opened the little wicket-gate wide, and Ivan stepped in.

Then they went to an upper room, where the bridegroom said to his bride, "When Koschei comes home, ask him where his death is."

Then Koschei came in through one door and Ivan went out through another door.

"*Phu! Phu!*" said Koschei Who Never Dies. "I smell the blood of a Russian. Was it Ivan Tsarevich who was with you just now, at this moment, and recently?"

"Why, Koschei Who Never Dies," said Peerless Beauty, clasping her hands, "Ivan Tsarevich has long ago been devoured by wild beasts of the plain. At least it must have been so and not otherwise."

They sat down to supper. When Koschei had eaten well and drunk better, Peerless Beauty said to him, "Tell me, now, Koschei, where is your death?"

"It's tied up in the broom, silly one," said Koschei. "Why do you wish to know?"

The next morning, Koschei Who Never Dies went out at the head of his men to fight. As soon as he'd gone, Ivan Tsarevich came to Peerless Beauty and kissed her sugar lips. Then she took the broom from the corner near the stove and gilded it all over with pure beaten gold. When this was done—and it took a long time to cover each twig of the birch boughs with the gold—Ivan left his bride.

Koschei Who Never Dies came in by another door. *"Phu! Phu!* I smell the blood of a Russian. Was it Ivan Tsarevich who was with you just now, at this moment, and recently?"

"Why, Koschei Who Never Dies," said Peerless Beauty clasping her hands, "you've been flying through Russia and have caught up the odor of the country on your own garments. How could I have seen Ivan Tsarevich?"

Then they sat down to supper. Koschei saw the gilded broom lying across the threshold. "What does this mean?" he asked sternly.

"See how I honor you," said Peerless Beauty, "for I gild even Death for you."

"Little simpleton, I fooled you," said Koschei.

"My death isn't in the broom. It's concealed in the oak fence."

The next day it happened as before. Peerless Beauty, helped by Ivan Tsarevich, gilded the fence. When Koschei saw it burning like fire in the evening sun, he laughed.

He said to Peerless Beauty, "Little simpleton, I fooled you. My death is in an egg, the egg is in a downy duck, and the duck is in the stump of a tree that floats upon the open sea."

The next day, Peerless Beauty rose quite early, before the sun was up, and went to the stove in the kitchen. "I must send Ivan Tsarevich," she said, "on the long search for that downy duck. He has a long way to go, so I must bake him a love cake."

She baked him not one love cake but three, and as she kneaded the dough, she spoke a love-spell into it, so that Ivan Tsarevich should fare well on his journey. The cakes were browned and buttered by the time Ivan came into the kitchen as the sun rose. Peerless Beauty had wrapped the cakes in a napkin of fine white linen, with edges of drawn thread-work. Then Ivan put his arms around the cake-baker, and she whispered into his ear where to look for the death of Koschei. And Ivan kissed her honey mouth and went out with the cakes in his pouch.

Onward he went and ever onward, until he came to the edge of the ocean. From there, he didn't know how to go farther. He'd eaten all the cakes and was famished, so hungry that when a hawk flew above his head, Ivan cried, "Hawk, hawk, I'll shoot you dead and eat you without cooking."

"Why eat me?" asked the hawk. "I can be of good service to you."

Then a great bear came shambling along with its fore-paws turned inwards to show that it was a bear of good breeding. "Bear, bear," said Ivan, "I'll shoot you dead and eat you without cooking."

"Why eat me?" asked the bear. "I can be of good service to you."

Then Ivan saw a great pike leap from the ocean and lie floundering on the shingle shore. "Pike, pike," said Ivan, "I'll kill you and eat you without cooking."

"Better, far better, and much the best," said the pike, "if you cast me into the sea."

"It seems to me," said Ivan Tsarevich, "that the cakes of Peerless Beauty have cast a spell, and I'm to have nothing more to eat. Well, then, with the strength of those cakes, I'll get on with it."

He flung the floundering pike back into the ocean. When it splashed, the great water boiled up and began to race along and up the shore so quickly that Ivan was forced to run before it with all his might.

Onward he ran and ever onward, with the water racing at his heels and occasionally washing over them. Onward he ran and ever upward, until he came to a tall tree on a high bank of sand. Upward he climbed and ever upward, and then saw that now the waters of the ocean were quickly falling. When they had gone back within their own boundaries, Ivan saw that they had left high up on the shore a huge stump of a tree.

The bear ran up, raised the stump in its arms, and hugged it until it cracked—*snap, smash*. From inside it, flew out a downy duck, which soared high and ever higher, until it looked like a dark green bottle with a long neck. Then the hawk flew up and caught it. At this point, an egg fell into the sea, but the pike caught it and swam to the beach, laying the egg gently at Ivan's feet.

The young man placed the egg in the warm napkin within his pouch and ran forward, ever forward, until he returned to Peerless Beauty, who was stooping over the kitchen stove. Ivan put his arms around the cake-baker, and she grasped his hands and pressed them. When she stood upright, the egg was in her left palm.

Ivan turned and saw Koschei sitting on the window ledge and scowling at him, because the dragon expected that the cakes and baked meats that Peerless Beauty was cooking were all for him. But as the dragon and man rushed to fight, Peerless Beauty dropped the egg onto the stove. It broke, and as the shell cracked, Koschei's heart broke also, and he fell down dead.

Then the bride and bridegroom went into the dining room, and Ivan Tsarevich feasted on cakes and baked meats, which Peerless Beauty had prepared while he was on his journey to the ocean. After that, they went to the country of Ivan's father.

Ivan's father rubbed his eyes when he saw them and said, "Why, Ivan Tsarevich left home when he was only nine days old. Now he brings Peerless Beauty to me as my daughter. Well, I never!"

"Well, we never!" cried the nurse-maidens in a chorus, as they ran to get ready for the second wedding, which was to be celebrated with great splendor. "Really, we never did! Whoever would have thought it?"

There is little doubt that Ivan Tsarevich was the first "nine days' wonder" that ever was.

# LITTLE ROLLING-PEA

*In a certain empire and a certain province, on the ocean sea, on the island of Bujan, stood a green oak, and under the oak a roasted ox, and by its side a sharpened knife. Suddenly, the knife was seized. Be so good as to eat! This isn't a story, but only a preface to a story. Whoever may listen to my story, may he have a sableskin cloak, and a horseskin cloak, and a beautiful woman, a hundred coins for the wedding, and fifty for a celebration!*

There was once a husband and wife. The wife went for water, took a bucket, and after drawing water, went home. On her way, she saw a pea rolling along.

She thought to herself, "This is a mysterious gift."

She picked up the pea and ate it. In due time, she became the mother of a baby boy, whom she named Little Rolling-pea. He grew not by years, but by hours, like millet dough when leavened. They nursed and pampered him in a way that couldn't be improved upon, and sent him to school. What others learned in three or four years, he understood in a single year, and the schooling was insufficient for him.

He came home from the school and said to his father and mother, "Now, then, daddy and mommy, thank my teachers, for already many have taught me, but now I know more than they."

He went into the street to amuse himself and found a pin, which he brought to his father and mother. He said to his father: "Here's a piece of iron. Take it to a smith, and let him make me a 250-pound mace from it."

His father didn't say a single word to him, but only thought, "My child is different from other people. I think he has a passable understanding, but now he's making a fool of me. How can a 250-pound mace be made out of a pin?"

His father, having a considerable sum of money in gold, silver, and paper, drove to the town, bought 250 pounds of iron and gave them to the smiths to make a mace. They made him a 250-pound mace, and the father brought it home. Little Rolling-pea came out from the attic, took his 250-

pound mace, and, hearing a storm approaching, threw the mace into the clouds.

He returned to his attic, and said, "Mother, look on my head before I go back outside. A nasty thing is biting me, for I am a young lad."

Rising from his mother's knees, he returned to the yard and looked at the clouds. Then he fell down with his right ear to the ground and listened. On rising, he called to his father, "Father, come here. See what is whizzing and humming? My mace is falling to the ground."

He placed his knee in the way of his mace. It struck him and broke in half.

He became angry with his father. "Father, why didn't you have a mace made for me out of the iron I gave you? If you had done so, it wouldn't have broken, but only bent. Here's the same iron for you. Go and get it made without adding any of your own."

The smiths put the iron into the fire and began to beat it with hammers and pull it until they made a 250-pound mace.

Little Rolling-pea took his 250-pound mace and got ready to go on a journey, a long journey. He walked and walked until he met a man.

"Greetings, brother Little Rolling-pea! Where are you going? Where are you traveling?"

Little Rolling-pea also asked him a question, "Who are you?"

"I'm the mighty hero Overturn-hill."

"Will you be my companion?" asked Little Rolling-pea.

He replied, "I'm at your service."

They went on together. They walked and walked until they met the mighty hero Overturn-oak.

"Greetings, brothers! Good health to you! Who are you?" asked Overturn-oak.

"Little Rolling-pea and Overturn-hill."

"Where are you going?"

"To such a city. A dragon devours people there, so we're going to kill him."

"May I join you?"

"You may join us," said Little Rolling-pea.

They went to the city and made themselves known to the emperor.

"What manner of men are you?" the emperor asked.

"We're mighty heroes!"

"Are you able to liberate this city? A ravenous dragon has been devouring many people. He must be killed."

"Why would we call ourselves mighty heroes, if we can't kill him?"

Midnight came, and the heroes approached a bridge of guelder-rose-wood that spanned a river of fire. A six-headed dragon rose from the river and stood on the bridge. Immediately, the dragon's horse neighed, his falcon screeched, and his hound howled.

The dragon gave his horse a blow on the head. "Don't neigh, devil's carrion! Don't screech, falcon! And you, hound, don't howl! For here is Little Rolling-pea," he said. "Come forward, Little Rolling-pea! Should we fight or only test our strength?"

Little Rolling-pea answered, "Good youths don't travel just to test their strength, but only to fight."

They began their combat. Little Rolling-pea and his companions each struck the dragon: three blows at a time on each of the three heads.

The dragon, realizing he couldn't escape destruction, said, "Well, brothers, it's only Little Rolling-pea that troubles me. I'll settle matters with you two."

They began to fight again, beat the dragon's remaining heads until he was dead. Little Rolling-pea cut out the tongues from all six heads, placed them in his knapsack, and tossed the headless body of the dragon into the river of fire. Then the heroes took the dragon's horse to the stable, his falcon to the courtyard, and his hound to the kennel. They returned to the emperor and brought him the tongues as proof the dragon was dead.

The emperor thanked them. "You are mighty heroes and deliverers of the city and all the people. If you wish to drink and eat, take whatever beverage and food you want without payment and without tax."

He joyfully proclaimed throughout the entire town that all the eating-houses, inns, and small public-houses were to be open for the mighty heroes. Well, they went everywhere, drank, amused themselves, refreshed themselves, and enjoyed various honors.

Night arrived, and exactly at midnight, the heroes went under the guelder-rose bridge to the river of fire. A seven-headed dragon quickly rose from the river. Immediately his horse neighed, his falcon screeched, and his hound howled.

The dragon struck his horse on the head. "Don't neigh, devil's carrion! Don't screech, falcon! Don't howl, hound! Here's Little Rolling-pea. Now then," said the dragon, "come forward, Little Rolling-pea! Should we fight or only test our strength?"

"Good youths don't travel to test their strength, but only to fight."

And they began their combat. The heroes beat six of the dragon's heads until they fell off; the seventh remained.

The dragon said, "Give me time to breathe!"

But Little Rolling-pea said, "Don't expect me to give you time to breathe."

They began their combat again. Little Rolling-pea beat off the final head, cut out the tongues, and placed them in his knapsack, but he threw the dragon's body into the river of fire. They returned to the emperor and brought the tongues as proof of the dragon's death.

The third time they went at midnight to the bridge of guelder-rose and the river of fire, a nine-headed dragon quickly rose to the surface. Immediately, his horse neighed, his falcon screeched, and his hound howled.

The dragon struck his horse on the head. "Don't neigh, devil's carrion! Don't screech, falcon! Don't howl, hound! Here's Little Rolling-pea. Come forward, Little Rolling-pea! Should we fight or only test our strength?"

Little Rolling-pea said, "Good youths don't travel just to test their strength, but only to fight."

They began their combat, and the heroes beat off eight heads; only the ninth remained.

Little Rolling-pea said, "Give us time to breathe, unclean beast!"

The dragon answered, "Take time to breathe or not. You won't overcome me. You killed my brothers by craftiness, not by strength."

Little Rolling-pea not only fought, but he wondered how to deceive the dragon. All at once, he thought of a plan, and said, "Yes, there's still much of your brother behind you. I'll fight you all."

Quickly, the dragon looked around, and Little Rolling-pea cut off the ninth head. He cut out the tongues, put them into his knapsack, and threw the body into the river of fire.

The heroes returned to the emperor, who said, "Thank you, mighty heroes! Live with joy and courage, and take as much gold, silver, and paper money as you desire."

After this, the wives of the three dragons met and decided what to do. "Where did those men come from who killed our husbands? What kind of women are we if we don't rid the world of the murderers?"

The youngest said, "Listen up, sisters! Let's go near the highway where the men will travel. I'll make myself into a beautiful roadside seat. If the men get tired, they'll sit on it. That will be death to them all."

The second said to her, "If you don't manage to harm them, I'll make myself into an apple tree beside the highway. When they approach me, the pleasant smell will attract them. Then, if they taste the apples, it will be death to them all."

Soon, the heroes approached the beautiful wayside seat. Little Rolling-pea thrust his sword into it up to the hilt, and blood poured out. They went on to the apple tree.

"Brother Little Rolling-pea," said the heroes, "let's each eat an apple."

But he said, "If it's possible, we'll eat; if it isn't possible, let's go on farther." He drew his sword and thrust it into the apple tree up to the hilt, and blood poured out immediately.

The third she-dragon hurried after them, and extended her jaws from the earth to the sky. Little Rolling-pea realized they didn't have room to pass by. How were they to save themselves? He looked around and saw that she especially looked at him, so he threw the three horses into her mouth. The she-dragon flew off to the blue sea to drink water, and the heroes proceeded on foot.

The she-dragon pursued them again. When Little Rolling-pea saw how near she was, he threw the three falcons into her mouth. Again, the she-dragon flew to the blue sea to drink water, and the heroes proceeded farther.

Little Rolling-pea looked round. The she-dragon was again pursuing him. Seeing the danger, he threw the three hounds into her mouth. Again, she flew off to the blue sea to drink water. While she drank her fill, the heroes proceeded still farther.

Little Rolling-pea looked around and saw that she was catching up with them again. Not knowing what else to do, he took his two comrades and threw them into her mouth. The she-dragon flew to the blue sea to drink water, and he went on alone.

Soon, the she-dragon overtook him. He looked around, but he didn't have anything left to throw into her mouth. He saw an iron workshop ahead of him and fled into the smithy.

The head smith said to him, "Why, stranger, are you behaving so cowardly?"

"Honorable gentlemen, protect me from an unclean beast!"

The smiths closed the smithy completely up.

"Give me what is mine!" said the she-dragon.

The smiths said to her, "Lick through the iron door, and we'll place him on your tongue."

She licked through the door and placed her tongue in the center.

Three at a time, the smiths seized her tongue with red-hot pincers and said, "Hurry, stranger, do with her what you will!"

Little Rolling-pea hurried out into the yard and beat the she-dragon. He pounded her skin to the bones, and her bones to the marrow. Then he buried her entire carcass seven fathoms deep.

*Then, and not until then, did he live and eat crumbs, but we ate bread, for he had none. I was there, too, and drank honey-wine. It flowed over my beard but didn't get into my mouth.*

# THE GOLDEN APPLES AND THE NINE PEAHENS

T here was once upon a time an emperor who had three sons. In his yard, a golden apple tree flowered and ripened every night, but somebody stole from it. The emperor had been utterly unable to discover the thief.

Once, he was talking with his sons and said to them, "I don't know where the fruit from our apple tree goes."

Then the eldest son answered him, "I'll stay tonight to see who takes it."

When it became dark, the eldest son did as he had said: went out and lay under the tree. When the apples began to ripen during the night, tiredness overtook him, and he fell asleep. He awoke at dawn and looked—but where were the apples? Taken away! When he saw this, he went and told everything to his father just as it happened.

The second son said to his father, "I'll watch tonight to see who takes it."

But he, too, watched it even as the first one. About the time when the apples began to ripen, he fell asleep. When he woke up in the morning, where were the apples? Taken away!

Now came the turn of the third and youngest brother. He went out at dusk under the apple tree, placed a sofa there, lay down, and went to sleep. About midnight, when the apples began to ripen, he woke up and looked at the apple tree. It had just begun to ripen and illuminated all the yard with the brightness of its fruit.

Just then up flew nine peahens, eight of which settled on the apple tree, and the ninth on the ground beside his sofa. As soon as she had landed, she became a woman, who shone with beauty like a bright sun. They talked together while the other eight were rifling the tree. When dawn came, she thanked him for the apples, and he begged her to leave just one behind. She gave him two—one for himself and one to take to his father—

transformed herself into a peahen, and flew away, followed by the other eight.

In the morning, the prince rose and took one apple to his father, who was overcome with joy and commended his son without ceasing. The next evening, the youngest prince went out again to watch the apple tree. As soon as he had gone out, he lay down as before and watched it that night also. In the morning, he again brought his father an apple.

This went on for a few days, when his brothers began to envy him, because they couldn't stay up to keep an eye on the tree, whereas he watched it successfully. They couldn't discover how he managed to stay awake. They sought out an old witch, who promised them to find out how their young brother guarded the apple tree.

At the approach of evening, when the youngest prince was about to go out to watch the apple tree, the accursed witch snuck out before him and lay under his sofa to conceal herself. The prince arrived, lay down without knowing the old woman was under his sofa, and went to sleep as previously. About midnight, when the prince had just woken up, the nine peahens arrived. Eight of them settled on the tree, and the other landed on the ground beside his sofa, transformed herself into a woman, and they began to talk together.

While these were conversing, the accursed old witch softly raised herself up and cut off a piece of the woman's long hair. As soon as she felt this, the damsel sprang away from the couch, transformed herself into a peahen, and flew away, with the other eight behind her.

The prince, on seeing this, leaped off his sofa and shouted, "What's happened?"

He soon caught sight of the old woman under the sofa, seized and hauled her from under it, and, when morning came, ordered her to be fastened to the tails of two horses and torn apart.

The peahens came no more to the apple tree. The prince grieved much on this account; he wept and mourned day after day. At last, he determined to search for them all over the world, and he told his father of his intentions.

His father tried to comfort him and said, "Stay, my son! I'll find you another woman in my empire, such a one you could ever wish for."

But it was in vain. The prince wouldn't listen to his father's advice. He made preparations to go. He took with him one of his servants and went into the world to find the peahen.

When he had traveled a long time, he came to a lake, in the midst of which was a rich palace, and in the palace an aged empress, who had one daughter. The prince, on approaching the old empress, asked her to tell him about the nine peahens, if she knew about them. The old woman replied that she did, and that the nine peahens came daily to bathe in the lake.

On telling him this, she tried to persuade him with these words: "Never mind those nine peahens, my son. I have a handsome daughter and an abundance of wealth—it could all be yours."

As soon as the prince heard where the peahens were, he wouldn't listen to the old woman talk. In the morning, he ordered his servant to get the horses ready to go to the lake.

Before they started for the lake, the old woman called his servant, bribed him, and gave him a little whistle, saying to him, "When the time approaches for the peahens to come to the lake, blow the whistle behind your master's neck. He'll immediately fall asleep and won't see them."

The accursed servant listened to her, took the whistle, and did as the old woman told him. When they arrived at the shore of the lake, he calculated the time when the peahens would arrive, blew the whistle behind his master's neck, and his master immediately fell as sound asleep as if he were dead. Scarcely had he fallen asleep when the peahens arrived. Eight of them settled on the lake.

The ninth perched on his horse and tried to awaken him: "Arise, my birdie! Arise, my lamb! Arise, my dove!"

He heard nothing, but slept on as if dead. When the peahens had finished bathing, they all flew away. The prince awoke and asked his servant, "What happened? Did they come?"

The servant replied, "They did come." He told the prince how eight of them settled on the lake, and the ninth on his horse, and that she tried to wake him.

When the unhappy prince heard this from his servant, he was despondent from pain and anger. The next morning, they visited the shore of the lake again, but his accursed servant calculated the time to blow the whistle behind the prince's neck, and the prince immediately fell asleep as if he were dead. Scarcely had he fallen asleep, when the nine peahens arrived. Eight settled on the lake, and the ninth on his horse.

She tried to awake him. "Arise, my birdie! Arise, my lamb! Arise, my dove!"

But he slept on as if he were dead, hearing nothing.

When the peahen failed to wake him, and they were about to fly away again, the one who had been trying to wake him turned and said to his servant, "When your master wakes, tell him that tomorrow it will once more be possible for him to see us, but after that, never more."

After saying this, she took flight, and the others from the lake after her.

Scarcely had they flown away, when the prince awoke, and asked his servant, "Did they come?"

He told him, "They did come, and eight of them settled on the lake, and the ninth on your horse, and tried to wake you, but you slept soundly. As she departed, she told me to tell you that you'll see her here once again tomorrow, and after that, never more."

When the prince heard this, he was depressed and didn't know what to do because of his sorrow. On the third day, he got ready to go to the lake, mounted his horse, went to the shore, and, in order not to fall asleep, kept his horse continually in motion. But his wicked servant, as he followed him, calculated the time, and blew the whistle behind the prince's neck, and the prince immediately leaned forward on his horse and fell asleep. As soon as he fell asleep, the nine peahens flew up; eight settled on the lake, and the ninth on his horse.

She endeavored to wake him. "Arise, my birdie! Arise, my lamb! Arise, my dove!"

But he slept as if he were dead and heard nothing.

Then, when they were about to fly away again, the one which had perched on his horse turned around and said to his servant, "When your master wakes up, tell him to roll the under peg on the upper, and then he will find me."

Then she flew off, and those from the lake after her.

When they had flown away, the prince awoke again and asked his servant, "Did they come?"

He replied, "They did, and the one that had perched on your horse told me to tell you to roll the upper peg on the under one, and then you would find her."[8]

When the prince heard this, he drew his sword and cut off his servant's head. Then he traveled alone. After he had travelled a long time, he came at dusk to a hermit's cottage and lodged there for the night.

In the evening, the prince asked the hermit, "Grandfather, have you heard of nine golden peahens?"

The hermit answered, "Yes, my son. You are fortunate in having come to me to ask about them. They're not far from here. It's not more than half a day's journey to them from here."

In the morning, when the prince departed to seek the peahens, the hermit came out to accompany him and said, "Go to the right, and you'll find a large gate. When you enter that gate, turn to the right. Then you'll go right into their town, and in that town is their palace."

---

[8] In the story, the servant switches the order around.

The prince went on his way according to the hermit's instructions. When he arrived at the gate, he turned to the right and saw the town on a hill. He was quite happy. When he entered the town, he asked where the palace of the nine peahens was. It was pointed out to him. At the gate, a watchman stopped him and asked where he'd come from and who he was. The prince told him everything, where he was from and who he was. After this, the watchman went off to announce the prince to the empress. When she heard it, she ran breathless and stood in the form of a woman before him, took him by the hand, and led him upstairs. Then the two rejoiced, and in a day or two were married.

A few days had elapsed after their marriage, and the empress prepared to go on a journey, while the prince remained alone. When she was about to start, she gave him keys to twelve cellars and said, "Open all the cellars, but stay away from the twelfth."

She went away, and the prince remained alone in the palace.

He thought, "What does this mean? I can open all the cellars, but not the twelfth? I wonder what's in it?"

He opened the doors one after the other. Finally, he came to the twelfth, and at first wouldn't open it.

As he had nothing else to do, though, he began to brood and to say to himself, "What can be in this cellar that she told me not to open it?"

At last, he opened it, too, and found standing in the middle of it a cask bound with iron hoops.

A voice cried out from it, saying, "Please, brother, I'm thirsty. Won't you give me a cup of water?"

On hearing the voice, the prince took a cup of water and sprinkled it on the stopper at the top of the cask. As soon as he had sprinkled it, one of the hoops of the cask burst.

The voice cried out again, "Give me one more cup of water, please. I'm still thirsty."

The prince sprinkled a second cup of water on the stopper. As soon as he had done so, the next hoop burst on the cask.

The voice then cried out a third time, "I'm still thirsty. Brother, please give me one more cup of water."

The prince poured another cup of water on the top of the cask. As soon as he had finished pouring it, the third hoop burst, the cask split open, and a dragon flew out of it. The dragon found the empress on her journey and carried her off. Thus it happened, and the attendants came and told their master that a dragon had carried the empress away.

The prince set off to seek her in the world. When he had travelled a long time, he came to a marsh, and in that marsh, he saw a little fish that was trying to jump into the water, but was unable to do so.

The little fish, on seeing the prince, addressed him, "Please, brother, do me a favor and throw me into the water. I'll help you out in return someday. Take a scale from me, and when you need me, rub it between your fingers."

On hearing this, the prince took a scale off it, threw the fish into the water, put the scale into a handkerchief, and went on his way. When he had gone a little farther, he saw a fox caught in a trap.

When the fox saw him, it called out, "Please, brother, let me out of this trap. I'll help you out in return someday. Take one or two hairs from my fur, and when you want me, rub them between your fingers."

The prince let the fox out of the trap, took one or two hairs from it, and went on his way. Thus, he proceeded onwards, until, as he went, he came to a hill, and found a crow caught in a trap just like the fox before.

As soon as the crow saw him, it cried out, "Please, be a brother to me, traveler, and release me from this trap. I'll help you out in return someday. Take a feather or two from me, and when you need me, rub them between your fingers."

The prince took one or two feathers from the crow, released it from the trap, and then went on his way.

As he went on to find the empress, he met a man and asked him, "Please, brother, tell me if you know where the palace of the dragon emperor is."

The man showed him the way and also told him when the dragon would be at home, so he might find him.

The prince thanked him and said, "Farewell."

He then went on and gradually reached the palace of the dragon emperor. On his arrival, he found his beloved. When she saw him and he saw her, they were both filled with joy and began to plan how to escape. Finally, they agreed to saddle their horses and take to flight. And so, they did just that: they saddled the horses, mounted, and off they fled.

When they had ridden off, the dragon arrived and looked around, but he couldn't find the empress. "What should we do?" said the dragon to his horse. "Should we eat and drink, or pursue them?"

The horse replied, "Don't trouble yourself; eat and drink first."

After the dragon had dined, he mounted his horse and galloped after them. He soon caught up and took the empress away.

He said to the prince, "You're safe this time. I'll forgive you, because you gave me water in the cellar. Don't attempt this a second time if your life is dear to you."

The poor prince remained thunderstricken. Finally, he regained his senses and started back home. He'd proceeded a little way, but since he couldn't overcome his heartache, he returned to the dragon's palace. There he found the empress weeping. When they saw each other, they again consulted about how to escape.

Then the prince said to the empress, "When the dragon returns, ask him where he bought that horse. Then tell me, so I can obtain another one. That's the only way we can escape."

After saying this to her, he left so the dragon wouldn't find him when the dragon returned. When the dragon came, the empress began to compliment him and make herself agreeable to him.

She said, "What a swift horse you have. Where did you buy him? Tell me, please."

He answered, "Where I bought him nobody can make a purchase. On a certain hill lives an old woman who has twelve horses in her stable, such creatures that you don't know which is better than the other. One of them is in the corner and looks skinny, but he's the best of all. He's the brother to my horse: this one can fly to the sky. Whoever seeks to obtain a horse from the old woman must serve her three days. The old woman has a mare with a foal. If the person can watch the mare successfully for three days and three nights, the old woman gives him the choice of whichever horse he wishes. If the person fails to watch the mare successfully for three days and three nights, he loses his life."

The next morning, the dragon went away, and the prince came in. The empress told him what the dragon had said. Then the prince started off and went to the hill to find the old woman.

When he entered her house, he said, "Good day, old woman!"

The old woman replied, "May you have prosperity, my son! What brings you here?"

He replied, "I'd like to work for you."

The old woman said, "Very well, my son. I have a mare with a foal. If you watch her successfully for three days, I'll give you one of my twelve horses, whichever one you want. Be warned, however, if you fail to watch her successfully, I'll take off your head."

Then she took him outside. In the yard, post after post was fixed in the ground, and on each was stuck a human head. Only one remained vacant, and this cried out continually, "Old woman, give me a head!"

When the old woman had shown the prince everything, she said, "I must tell you that all these men engaged me to watch the mare and the foal, but none were able to watch her successfully."

But the prince was in no way terrified. In the afternoon, he mounted the mare and galloped uphill and downhill, with the foal galloping after them. The prince did this until midnight. At that point, weariness crept over him, and he fell asleep.

He woke up at dawn. His arms were around a stump instead of the mare, but he held the halter in his hand. When he realized the mare was gone, the poor fellow became dizzy from terror and started looking for her. In his searching, he came to a pool of water, and that reminded him of the little fish. He unfolded the handkerchief, removed the scale, and rubbed it between his fingers. Up sprang the little fish out of the water and lay before him.

"What's the matter, adopted brother?" said the fish.

The prince replied, "The old woman's mare has escaped from me, and I don't know where she is."

The fish said to him, "Here she is among us. She's transformed herself into a fish, and her foal into a little fish. All you have to do to get her back is flap the halter on the water and call out, 'Coop! Coop! Old woman's mare!' "

The prince flapped the water with the halter and called out, "Coop! Coop! Old woman's mare!" and immediately she transformed herself again into a mare, and, *pop!* there she was on the edge of the water before him!

He put the halter on her and mounted her, and *trot! trot!* back they went to the old woman's house. When he brought her back, the old woman gave the prince his dinner.

She led the mare into the stable, scolded her, and said, "Among the fish, good-for-nothing rogue?"

The mare replied, "I was among the fish, but they told on me, because they're his friends."

The old woman said to her, "Go among the foxes."

The second day, the prince mounted the mare and galloped uphill and downhill, with the foal galloping after them. The prince did this until midnight, at which time weariness overcame him, and he fell asleep on the mare's back.

At dawn, when he awoke, his arms were around a stump, but he held the halter in his hand. When he realized this, he sprang off again to seek her. As he was looking for her, he remembered what the old woman had said to the mare as she was leading it into the stable. He unwrapped the fox's hairs out of the handkerchief, rubbed them between his fingers, and the fox immediately jumped out before him.

"What is it, adopted brother?"

The prince replied, "The old woman's mare has run away."

The fox said to him, "Here she is among us. She's become a fox, and the foal a fox-cub. All you have to do to get her back is flap the ground with the halter, and call out, 'Coop! Coop! Old woman's mare!' "

The prince flapped and called, and the mare leaped out before him. He caught her and put the halter on her, mounted her, and rode to the old woman's house. When he brought the mare home, the old woman gave the prince his dinner.

The old woman led the mare off to the stable and said, "Among the foxes, good-for-nothing rogue?"

The mare replied, "I was among them, but they're his friends and told on me."

The old woman said to her, "Be among the crows."

The third day, the prince again mounted the mare and galloped her uphill and downhill, with the foal galloping after them. The prince did this until midnight, when weariness finally overcame him, and he fell asleep. He woke up at dawn, but his arms were around a stump, and he held the halter in his hand.

As soon as he realized this, he darted off again to look for the mare. Then, he remembered what the old woman had said the day before when scolding the mare. He took out the handkerchief and unwrapped the crow's feathers, rubbed them between his fingers, and, *pop!* the crow was before him.

"What is it, adopted brother?"

The prince replied, "The old woman's mare has run away, and I don't know where she is."

The crow answered, "Here she is among us. She's become a crow, and the foal a young crow. All you have to do to get her back is flap the halter in the air and cry, 'Coop! Coop! Old woman's mare!' "

The prince flapped the halter in the air and cried, "Coop! Coop! Old woman's mare!"

The mare transformed herself from a crow into a mare, just as she had been, and came before him. He put the halter on her, mounted her, and galloped off, the foal following behind, to the old woman's house. The old woman gave the prince his dinner.

She caught the mare, led her into the stable, and said to her, "Among the crows, good-for-nothing rogue?"

The mare replied, "I was among them, but they're his friends and told on me."

Then, when the old woman came back to the house, the prince said to her, "Well, old woman, I've served you honestly. Now I ask you to give me that which we agreed on."

The old woman replied, "My son, what is agreed on must be given. Here are twelve horses. Choose whichever you please."

He replied, "Which should I pick and choose? Give me that one in the corner; there's none better in my eyes."

Then the old woman tried to persuade him otherwise. "Why choose that skinny one when there are so many good ones?"

He insisted. "Give me the one I asked for; that was our agreement."

The old woman twisted, turned, and without more ado, gave him the one he asked for.

The prince mounted the horse and called out, "Farewell, old woman!"

"Good-bye, my son!"

When he took the horse into the woods and groomed it, the creature glittered like gold. Afterwards, when he mounted it and gave it free rein, it flew, flew like a bird, and in a jiffy arrived at the dragon's palace.

As soon as he entered the courtyard, he told the empress to get ready for flight. She wasn't long in getting ready. They both mounted the horse and set off.

They hadn't been gone long when the dragon arrived home and looked about. No empress.

Then he said to his horse, "Should we eat and drink, or should we pursue?"

"Eat or not, drink or not, pursue or not, you won't catch him."

When the dragon heard this, he immediately mounted his horse and pursued them.

By and by, the prince and empress realized the dragon was pursuing them. They were terrified and urged their horse to go quickly.

The horse answered them, "Never fear. There's no need to hurry."

The dragon came *trot, trot*, and the horse he rode called out to the one that carried the prince and the empress, "Bless you, brother, wait! I'm out of breath from pursuing you."

The other horse replied, "Whose fault is that? You're such a fool to carry that specter on your back. Buck and throw him to the ground and then follow me."

When the dragon's horse heard this, up with his head, a jump with his hind-quarters, and *bang* went the dragon against a stone. The dragon was smashed to pieces, and his horse followed the prince and empress. The empress caught and mounted it, and they arrived safe and sound in the empress's dominions.

They reigned honorably as long as they lived.

# About the Author

Ronesa Aveela is "the creative power of two." Two authors that is. Nelly, the main force behind the work, the creative genius, was born in Bulgaria and moved to the US in the 1990s. She grew up with stories of wild Samodivi, Kikimora, the dragons Zmey and Lamia, Baba Yaga, and much more. She's a freelance artist and writer. She likes writing mystery romance inspired by legends and tales. In her free time, she paints. Her artistic interests include the female figure, Greek and Thracian mythology, folklore tales, and the natural world interpreted through her eyes. She is married and has two children.

Rebecca, her writing partner was born and raised in the New England area. She has a background in writing and editing, as well as having a love of all things from different cultures. She's learned so much about Bulgarian culture, folklore, and rituals, and writes to share that knowledge with others.

**Connect with us at** www.ronesaaveela.com.

If you'd like to learn more about dragons, check out our nonfiction book called *A Study of Dragons of Eastern Europe*,
https://books2read.com/dragons-aveela.

Would you like to learn more about folklore and mythology? Sign up for our newsletter and receive a FREE supplement to our "Spirits and Creatures" book series about a malicious water spirit: Vodyanoy or Vodnik. Link to download: https://bit.ly/2XHovX8

# Reviews

We hope you've enjoyed this book, and that its stories have inspired you. We would appreciate your gift of a review. Good or bad, we'd love to hear your honest thoughts.

# Artist Profile

**Keazim Issinov**, whose painting we've used with permission for this book's cover, was born in the village of Sadovets, Pleven region, on April 16, 1940. He graduated from the National Art School in 1960, and in 1968 graduated from The National Academy of Art, the class of Prof. Nenko Balkanski in Painting. After graduation he worked as a restorer at the Institute of National Monuments of Culture. In 1969 he started work at the National Research Institute of Psychology and Neurology as an art teacher. During his fifty years of creative work, the author has won many awards and participated in Bulgaria and abroad in many events, connected with charity.

2005: Awarded Artist of the Century in the competition Millennium "1001 Reasons to Love the Earth" held in the Netherlands.

2015: Awarded by the Ministry of Culture the Order "Golden Age."

Although Keazim's thematic range includes a series of paintings dedicated to the great masters of European art, as well as to man's connection with nature, his priority remains Christian art, in particular icon art. It has left its mark on the inner light they emit, in the density of brown and fiery red, in the silvery and blue-green tones of the landscapes as a whole, typically giving off its colorful magical polyphony. The retrospective of Keazim's work once again explains his nickname of "enthusiastic pantheist," standing out even more in today's naked and orphaned by ideas, dreams and utopias, world.

Facebook: https://www.facebook.com/issinov

# STORY SOURCES

Original sources of stories in order of appearance:

Fillmore, Parker. "Vitazko the Victorious," 59-88. In *The Shoemaker's Apron; a Second Book of Czechoslovak Fairy Tales and Folk Tales*. New York: Harcourt, Brace and Howe, 1920. https://hdl.handle.net/2027/nyp.33433021210293.

Curtin, Jeremiah. "Miklosh and the Magic Queen," 120-140. In *Fairy Tales of Eastern Europe*. New York: R. M. McBride, 1931. https://hdl.handle.net/2027/uc1.$b41194.

Fillmore, Parker. "Batcha and the Dragon," 149-163. In *The Shoemaker's Apron; a Second Book of Czechoslovak Fairy Tales and Folk Tales*. New York: Harcourt, Brace and Howe, 1920. https://hdl.handle.net/2027/nyp.33433021210293.

Curtin, Jeremiah. "The Laughing Apples and the Weeping Quinces," 227-242. In *Fairy Tales of Eastern Europe*. New York: R. M. McBride, 1931. https://hdl.handle.net/2027/uc1.$b41194.

Ralston, William. "Ivan Popyalof," 66-70. In *Russian Folk-tales*. London: Smith, Elder, 1873. https://hdl.handle.net/2027/uc1.31158010565728.

Stăncescu, Dumitru. "Împăratul Peştilor" [The emperor of the fish], 245-257. In *Basme, culese din gura poporului* [Fairy tales, collected from the mouths of the people]. Bucuresci: Haimann, 1892. https://hdl.handle.net/2027/hvd.32044019182302.
Note: This story also appears in our book *A Study of Dragons of Eastern Europe*.

Curtin, Jeremiah. "Dawn, Twilight, and Midnight," 15-23. In *Fairy Tales of Eastern Europe*. New York: R. M. McBride, 1931. https://hdl.handle.net/2027/uc1.$b41194.

Mügge, Maximilian A. "The Castle in Cloudland," 117-121. In *Serbian Folk Songs: Fairy Tales and Proverbs*. London: Drane's, [1916]. https://hdl.handle.net/2027/mdp.39015008931480. **Also**: Petrovitch, Woislav M. "A Pavilion Neither in the Sky nor on the Earth," 220-224. In *Hero Tales and Legends of the Serbians*. New York: Stokes [1915]. https://hdl.handle.net/2027/uc1.$b98107.

Houghton, Louise Seymour. "The Seven Stars," 129-135. In *The Russian Grandmother's Wonder Tales*. New York: C. Scribner's Sons, 1913. https://hdl.handle.net/2027/uc1.$b41190.

Curtin, Jeremiah. "The World-beautiful Sharkan Roja," 79-90. In *Fairy Tales of Eastern Europe*. New York: R. M. McBride, 1931. https://hdl.handle.net/2027/uc1.$b41194.

Curtin, Jeremiah. "Ivan the Peasant's Son and the Little Man Himself One-finger Tall, His Mustache Seven Verts in Length," 37-46. In *Myths and Folk-tales of the Russians, Western Slavs, and Magyars*. London: Sampson Low, Marston, Searle & Rivington, 1890. https://hdl.handle.net/2027/ucw.ark:/13960/t0wq0g13s.

"Змей и цыган." [A Russian folk tale collected by A.N. Afanasyev.] https://ru.wikisource.org/wiki/Народные_русские_сказки_(Афанасьев) /Змей_и_цыган.

Wilson, Richard. "Peerless Beauty the Cake-Baker," 291-307. In *The Russian Story Book*. London: Macmillan, 1916. https://hdl.handle.net/2027/mdp.39015002199639.

Wratislaw, A. H., M.A., trans. "Little Rolling-pea," 132-138. In *Sixty Folk-tales from Exclusively Slavonic Sources*. London: Elliot Stock, 1889. https://hdl.handle.net/2027/uc1.$b282186.

Wratislaw, A. H., M.A., trans. "The Golden Apples and the Nine Peahens," 186-198. In *Sixty Folk-tales from Exclusively Slavonic Sources*. London: Elliot Stock, 1889. https://hdl.handle.net/2027/uc1.$b282186.

Printed by BoD"in Norderstedt, Germany